Flint

Book 2:

Working Girls

Flint

Book 2:

Working Girls

Treasure Hernandez

www.urbanbooks.net

Urban Books, LLC
78 East Industry Court
Deer Park, NY 11729

ISBN 13: 978-1-60162-122-1
ISBN 10: 1-60162-122-1

First Trade Paperback Printing June 2008
First Mass Paperback Printing May 2010
Printed in the United States of America

10   9   8   7   6   5   4   3

Distributed by Kensington Publishing Corp.
Submit Wholesale Orders to:
Kensington Publishing Corp.
C/O Penguin Group (USA) Inc.
Attention: Order Processing
405 Murray Hill Parkway
East Rutherford, NJ 07073-2316
Phone: 1-800-526-0275
Fax: 1-800-227-9604

ACKNOWLEDGMENTS

First and foremost, I'd like to thank God for all the blessings He has bestowed upon me.

I would like to thank the Urban Books staff: Smiley, Lonnie, Denard, Aiesha, Natalie and Nicole. And as always Mr. Carl Weber. I would also like to thank all the Urban Books fans for supporting all the creative African-American writers.

Most of all I would like to thank all my positive and strong sisters who unfortunately have been stripped of their freedom and families. As Pac would say *"Keep your head up"* and *"Dear Mamas."*

We will be free again. Holla!

Treasure Hernandez
c/o Urban Books
1199 Straightpath
West Babylon, NY 11704

Love & Peace,

Treasure

Chapter One

"Take it or leave it, mu'fucka. It is what it is." Malek held one hand in his pants and looked up the block to make sure the coast was clear as he interacted with the dope fiend. "You can take yo' ass over to the South Side and cop some of that bullshit dope if you want to, or be satisfied with what I just gave your ass." Malek waited for his customer to respond, although he knew that eventually the man would see things his way, because Jamaica Joe had the best connect in the city of Flint.

The dope fiend examined the bag of heroin, holding it up high and thumbing it in an attempt to make all of the contents fall to the bottom. He could get a better picture of just how much dope he had if it was all heaped together in one pile. The fiend had been complaining about the pack's size. Whether Malek obliged his complaint or not, he knew that he had the best dope in town in the palm of his hands and he wasn't going to pass up that good high for nothing. The customer nodded with approval and then walked off after leaving Malek with fifty dollars, of course, and took the bag of dope with him.

Malek sat on the stoop as he waited for his next customer. He wouldn't be surprised if it turned out to be the same fiend that had just walked off. Ever since Malek started slinging that premium, the term "repeat customer" had a new definition. Hell, some fiends would only get as far as their automobile, smoke up their dope, then hit Malek right back up again. It was crazy like that.

As Malek sat waiting, all types of thoughts crossed his mind, but not for one moment did he think about how quickly he had gone from becoming a potential NBA star athlete to a fuckin' corner boy. Standing six feet and five inches tall, Malek was built for the NBA, but when his mother and stepfather were killed in a drive-by shooting, his dream of having a basketball career died with them. They had been his strength, his rock, his reason for wanting it so bad. They had sacrificed their entire lives for him, and Malek wanted nothing more than to reward their efforts by seeing to it that, through his skills and talents, they would never need to work again a day in their lives.

Malek was in the hospital recovering from two bullet wounds he had suffered at the Berston Park Battle annual basketball game when he'd learned of his parents' fate. Bullets from a drive-by shooting had riddled his house, killing his mother, who was walking up the porch steps, heading home after spending days in the hospital by his side. They also killed his stepfather, who lay asleep on the front living room couch. It had only been hours prior to their deaths when Malek learned of the death of his opportunity to enter the NBA draft; his agent had dropped him like he had never known him. He hadn't even had the decency to tell Malek himself. He sent the message through Malek's mother, who it pained tremendously to be the bearer of bad news. The agent didn't even have the decency to come to his parents' funeral after all the times his mother had spent hours preparing meals for him while they discussed Malek's future career. Malek learned that in this world, just as soon as you no longer have that thing that person is trying to get out of you, they don't know you anymore. Unfortunately, he hadn't learned this lesson only from his agent.

When Malek was released from the hospital, he had nowhere to go. He was of adult age, but he was still in high school. How in the hell was he supposed to pay the house note that his parents had left behind? He got a little bit of change from a life insurance policy his parents had, but after he gave them a proper burial, there was hardly enough money left to pay for a night at a hotel, let alone pay a mortgage. It wasn't long before the bank foreclosed on the house and Malek ended up on the streets.

With no other family in Flint, Malek turned to the one source that always seemed to be a last option; one that doesn't discriminate . . . the streets. With a broken spirit and broken dreams, it wasn't long before Malek fell into the street life full force. Jamaica Joe, whose street credentials were much validated on the streets of Flint, took Malek under his wing and put him on the block in search of the American dream. Now that it was obvious that his basketball talents weren't going to get him in the pros, Malek was getting money the only way he knew how.

Although Malek's bullet wounds might not have been life-threatening, one just happened to bury itself in his leg. He had barely been checked into the hospital before NBA teams, and even colleges, lost interest in him. He knew he didn't have a chance in the world when even his agent abandoned him in the hospital bed. They all feared the inevitable: that his leg would never allow him to play ball like he once did before the ill-fated shooting. He now walked with a very slight limp, which he camouflaged as part of a smooth swagger.

Malek took to the streets like a duck took to water, and it turned out that he was a natural-born hustler. Anyone who knew him in high school would never have guessed it. He had always managed to keep his nose clean and stay focused. He never hung around the wrong crowd and had managed to maintain average grades without the perks some teachers gave a couple of the other ball players. His mind stayed on his ultimate goal: becoming a pro baller. But now . . . he was a baller all right.

He had only been hustling for a year, but quickly moved up in the ranks. Joe had given him his own block in the Fifth Ward, which was the most profitable block on the North Side of Flint.

Every day Malek thought about his mother and stepfather and missed them dearly. To date, the police had not found the person responsible for the fatal shootings, and that hurt him even more. Revenge and hatred toward the unknown perpetrator was buried in his bones, just waiting to be resurrected. The shooter had taken away every person he had ever loved. Almost everybody, with the exception of Halleigh, who just seemed to walk away on her own free will, left Malek for dead, it seemed.

Halleigh was about the only girl Malek had ever loved. As a matter of fact, it was the night that he had decided to keep his promise to her and stand by her side and be there for her that his entire life changed for the worse. And yet, it seemed she hadn't so much as thought twice about him since. He had put his entire life on the line and ruined it for her; someone who didn't even love him back enough to come see about him in the hospital after the shooting. At the end of the day, Malek had to admit that losing Halleigh hurt more than losing his dreams.

Malek rubbed his neck, which had his deceased mother's name tattooed on it, as he scanned the block. When he saw a silver Lexus turning the corner, he smiled and threw his hands up, knowing that it was Joe. The car pulled up and stopped in front passenger's side of Malek. The back passenger's side window rolled down. As always, Joe sat in the passenger's seat while his head henchman, Tariq, chauffeured him around.

Tariq didn't mind that part of his job at all. Everyone in the game knew that he was more than just some driver. He was Joe's right hand man; next in line when and if Joe ever decided to retire from the game. If anything, it was more of an honor than a duty.

"What's good, son?" Joe asked as he rolled down the window and looked at Malek.

Malek walked over to the car and extended his hand to show Joe love. "What up, fam?" he replied, greeting Joe with a handshake and a snap.

"Get in." Joe threw his head in the direction of the empty seat next to him.

Malek walked around to the other side, opened the door, and slid in next to Joe. When Malek got in, Tariq gave him an envious stare through the rearview mirror.

Although he had never verbally expressed it, Tariq didn't care for Malek too much. It was safe to say that he was a little envious of how his boss had taken to the youngster, putting his trust and loyalty in this kid so quickly. The fact that after only a year Malek was running his own block was evidence that. For some reason, Joe favored this young buck. Tariq had to be a corner boy for years before Joe gave him his own block. So he had envy in his heart toward Malek, who moved up in the ranks after only a few months of putting in work, not just for Joe, but in the game, period. And for Malek to have the busiest block of them all only added to Tariq's jealousy.

Joe lit his blunt while they sat in the idle car. He

took a puff and then asked Malek, "How you do this week?"

"I need to re-up again," Malek said as he spotted one of his workers and waved him over.

Trap, a heavyset hustler about the same age as Malek, scanned the block and then reached under the porch of the house he sold from and grabbed a brown paper bag. He then ran over to the car and handed it to Malek. Malek took the bag, opened it, looked inside and then turned and handed it to Joe.

Joe opened the bag to see money rolls filling it up to the top. A smile crept across his face as he nodded proudly. Through the rearview mirror, Tariq watched, boiling inside, knowing that this kid was about to receive accolades from the boss.

Joe closed the bag and set it in between him and Malek. Shaking his head, he said to Malek, "You never cease to amaze me, Malek."

The compliment made Malek feel good as Joe spoke to him just as proudly as his stepfather would have congratulated him on winning the NBA championship.

"If you keep this up, you're going to be great in this game," Joe added, referring to the dope game.

Joe had never seen anyone move dope like Malek moved it. From the moment Joe had first seen Malek in that county jail cell, he knew this kid had a bigger hustle in him than the petty crime he was being held for. His instincts had steered him right, because the way Malek had been putting in work lately, Joe knew that without a doubt, just like himself, Malek was born to hustle.

Once again, just like it had with Tariq, Joe's intuition that he could benefit greatly if Malek's services paid off; and the service went beyond the initial one of Malek just winning a basketball game for him.

It was at Berston Park, where Joe, with fifty grand at stake, convinced Malek to play on his North Side team in the basketball game when the youngin's skills first paid off for Joe. Against Malek's agent's wishes, Malek agreed to play on Joe's team, not because he wanted to, but because he felt obligated. After all, Joe was the one who'd hired that infamous Flint "street attorney" who got Malek out of jail for robbery. It was a robbery he wouldn't have even thought to attempt in his wildest dreams had it not have been for Halleigh.

Thanks to Malek's basketball skills, Joe's team won the game indeed, but that only pissed off his lifelong enemy, Sweets, who ran the South Side team, and who lost his fifty Gs to Joe, plus bragging rights he had victoriously retained for the past four games. Not to mention his pride. In retaliation, an all-out North Side/South Side war broke out after the game. Malek, once again, came to Joe's rescue, taking two bullets that were intended for Joe.

Malek remained silent as he took in Joe's compliments. He glanced up at Tariq, who was mugging him through the mirror.

What's that niggas problem? Malek thought as he returned a mean stare for a brief moment. Malek felt an uneasiness around Tariq. Not that he was a threat or anything; Malek just sensed that Tariq was lightly offended by his presence. Malek knew that because he was so young, the older cats who had been in the game would be intimidated by a young hustler getting his grind on. But that never stopped Malek from doing what he had to do. What Malek did sometimes worry about was another hatin'-ass nigga trying to stop him.

I'm going to have to keep an eye on that nigga Tariq, Malek surmised. *He might just be a problem.*

Joe interrupted Malek's thoughts. "You ran through a whole brick in two days?" Joe asked him, not believing the obvious.

"Yeah. That shit is like clockwork 'round here. I be hittin' niggas off proper. I don't be cutting my shit heavy." Malek shared with Joe his technique that kept the fiends coming back. "I might not make as much on the flip, but I run through the dope faster, re-upping more. So, in the long run, I make more money."

"If more mu'fuckas thought like you, then everybody could eat off this game." Joe looked to his head henchman. "Ain't that right, Tariq? Not even your ass ever came up with that type of logic." He turned his attention back to Malek, leaving Tariq's ego wounded. "Niggas get greedy and try to stretch they dope so much that it doesn't even get their customers high anymore." Joe inhaled the smoke into his lungs. "I'll have someone drop off a brick in an hour."

"No doubt," Malek said. He then immediately turned the conversation to some more important business. "Have you found out anything about the shooting?" he asked Joe for the millionth time. Joe had promised Malek that he would look into the random drive-by shooting that took his mother's and stepfather's lives a year earlier. Joe told Malek that niggas in the street talked; they were worse than broads sometimes. He assured him that he would have his soldiers keep their ears to the street and he would find out just exactly who was behind it. And when they did, payback would be a mutha.

Joe's reassurance wasn't enough for Malek. Time was of the essence. The spirit of revenge was embedded deep inside Malek's bones. Every day that went by was another day that the culprit got to breathe. And Malek wasn't having that. So every time he got a chance, he asked Joe that very same question. He was worse than Celie in *The Color Purple*, asking Mister every day if any mail had come for her.

"No, not yet, but trust me, I am going to handle that for you. We're going to make whoever did that pay," Joe answered.

"Yeah, I hear you, man," Malek said as he exited the car.

Joe could hear the disappointment and doubt in Malek's tone. "Don't worry. We gon' find that shit out. You feel me?" Malek gave a doubtful nod. "You trust me on this one?"

Malek stood outside of the car and looked up to the heavens, where he knew that as much as his mother loved and served the Lord, she was watching down on him. He then looked back down at Joe. "Yeah, I trust you, man."

"That's what I'm talking about." Joe stuck out his hand to give Malek some dap and then signaled for Tariq to drive off.

Ever since the death of Malek's parents, Joe and Malek had formed a close bond. After losing all potential to go pro, Malek fell into the arms of the streets. With Joe there grooming him, he rose up in the dope game swiftly and began to make a name for himself in the drug game instead of the basketball game.

Malek had once been popular at his high school, though he never even managed to graduate after all that stuff went down with the robbery, jail and the shootings. Instead, he made money hustling, dedicating his life to the streets. Now turned out by the streets, there was no turning back for Malek. He was deep into the game now, and everybody knew that there were only two ways out: death or jail. So now it was all about the survival of the fittest, and he was in for keeps.

Chapter Two

Halleigh waited inside the hotel room for her next john to show up. Tasha usually sent the men into the room one after another. On that particular day, though, business was slow. Halleigh wasn't complaining. She needed the break. Her body was tired from the constant sexing of men over the last year.

She sat in front of the vanity mirror, and tears began to flow as she looked into her soulless pupils. She hated the woman that she'd become. She had once been a plain Jane high school honors student with a positive future. She was even dating what the world thought was a shoo-in future NBA star. No one would believe—hell, she didn't believe—that that same girl was now selling her body and her soul to any man with the right amount of cash.

Her mascara ran down her cheeks as she reached

into her blouse and pulled out a small plastic baggie. She emptied the contents of the baggie onto the vanity table and made it into a straight line with her pinky fingernail. Halleigh looked down at the white substance that had become her "acquaintance" over the last six months. She'd started snorting as an escape from the reality she was living, hoping that, like Calgon, the feeling would take her away; that it wouldn't be her laying there while every Tom, Dick, and Kwalie got on top of her and did their business.

Halleigh couldn't believe she was heading down the same path of drug abuse as her fiended-out mother, Sharina, whom she hadn't seen since Sharina had allowed two thugs to take Halleigh's virginity just for a hit. Halleigh had heard of drug addicts selling off their kids just to get high, but she never thought in her worst nightmare that she would be the victim of such an act.

The brutal assault left Halleigh devastated. Her own mother had turned on her, sitting in the next room getting high while Halleigh cried out and fought, to no avail, to protect her innocence and escape from the clutches of the attackers. So afterwards, with nowhere else to turn, she went to where she thought she would be safe and protected. She went to Malek. Her high school sweetheart had promised to take care of her. He said he wouldn't let anything happen to her before getting her up out of the hood. But look at her now. Not only was she still in the hood, but Malek wasn't there for her.

"I hate my life. It wasn't supposed to be like this," Halleigh whispered as she lowered her head and sniffed the cocaine into her nostrils. She immediately jerked her head back to prevent her nose from running. She had picked up this bad habit from a john she serviced frequently. He'd convinced her that the drug was an escape, the much-needed escape her mind had been desiring. She needed to escape from the pain. She needed to escape from life itself.

After her initial introduction to the vice, she had developed a steady habit for the drug. Whenever she was feeling down or needed a boost to cope with her profession, she leaned on her "new friend," cocaine. She had to admit, ever since she started using the drug, her clientele had picked up and became more regular. High on coke, she got lost in herself, in the moment, willing to do things that she would not have done otherwise. Sexual exploration was like a side effect of the drug.

The phone rang, startling Halleigh as she was trying to enjoy her high. She wiped her runny nose and walked over to the phone.

"Hello?" she sniffed.

"You got another john coming up. He wants a number two," Tasha said, referring to vaginal sex. They called oral sex *number one* and vaginal sex *number two. Twelve* was the total package, meaning the client paid double for anything his heart desired, or on some occasions, her heart desired.

The business of trickin' wasn't just exclusive for men out to throw away some cash for a few moments of pleasure. There were female clients every now and then also. A couple of the women were married with children, but secretly had desires to be with other women. They didn't want to chance getting into a serious relationship with a woman and being found out, so this was the only other way they could think to cure the craving inside of them.

One time Halleigh had two female clients at once. Fortunately, all they wanted Halleigh to do was watch them. But another time, when they showed up as repeat customers and were assigned to Mimi, they wanted the third wheel to roll with them. Of course, Mimi didn't play when it came to gettin' money, so she was down for whatever. Every act had a price tag on it as far as she was concerned.

Halleigh took a deep breath and shook her head from side to side. She was sore, worn-out, and needed a while to recoup. Her last client had paid for a number twelve and she thought he'd never leave. But as long as the money kept coming, no pun intended, Halleigh had to keep him comin'.

Halleigh sighed as a stalling technique. "Tash, I just came on my period. I can't do it," Halleigh lied, trying to avoid having to take the job. Not even high off the cocaine could she force her body to cooperate with the next trick's request.

What Halleigh failed to realize was that as the madam, Tasha made it her business to know every single girl's cycle like clockwork. She even had a calendar; that way she knew to send the johns who only wanted oral sex performed on them to the girls who were on their periods. So she was very much aware of the fact that Halleigh's period wasn't due for a week or so. Just to double check, though,

Tasha opened her calendar in the back of her appointment book and scanned down until she found Halleigh's name.

"What you talking about, Hal? You know and I know that you ain't on the rag yet," Tasha replied in a confident tone after verifying such on her calendar. "Don't even try that bullshit. Trust me, many a girl before you have tried that same lame-ass excuse. There is no time for laziness. In this business, a girl's gotta put her stilettos on and hustle-hustle." Tasha snapped her finger twice. "This is about making that dough. And you know what happens when someone tries to fuck with Manolo's cash flow. Now, with all that said, do you want that trick's dick up in your pussy, or Daddy's foot up in your ass?"

Halleigh knew that Tasha was right. Manolo didn't deviate from the reputation pimps were known to have. He was as smooth as silk when he wanted to be, convincing a chick to sell her pussy and give him the money. But he was known for his short temper with the girls when it came to fucking up his money or just simply being disobedient and not following the rules. Manolo didn't mind making an example out of any one of the girls so that the next chick wouldn't get any ideas and try to follow suit.

Halleigh thought about that time when she'd first started in the business and Manolo had beaten her down after she refused to please him orally. Then, just like now, she had been worn out and tired after spending an entire day with johns. But even as she reflected back on the beating, as tired as she was now, she thought the beat-down just might be worth it.

"My body has been acting funny lately. I haven't been getting a lot of rest, Tash. You know that," Halleigh replied in a whiny voice, hoping to gain her madam's sympathy.

Tasha felt bad for Halleigh and knew that she needed a break, but she also knew that Manolo would have a problem with that and take it out on Halleigh's ass. If it wasn't for Tasha coming to her rescue that time Manolo beat Halleigh, the nineteen-year-old might not even be alive today. Tasha couldn't help but fear what would happen if Manolo got a hold of her again and she wasn't there to protect her this time.

"Look, you can take the rest of the day off and get yourself together," Tasha told her, "but you have to stay in the room so Manolo won't find out. I'll send your clients to some of the other girls."

"Thank you so much, Tash. I owe you." Halleigh was glad that she had found favor in Tasha's sight.

When Halleigh first started working for Manolo, she saw Tasha as some hardcore, unfeeling broad who cared about two things only—Manolo and Manolo. This meant that she carried the whip, making sure that bitches followed his orders so that he stayed happy, and that no bitch tried to take her place. Getting paid and taken care of without giving up the pussy was a position Tasha was not willing to give up. On top of that, she got five percent profit off of whatever the girls made for Manolo. Being the madam over the Manolo Mamis definitely had its perks.

"Oh, please believe, you still working today. I'm

just not going to send you any clients. I need you to make store runs for me today. So come next door and get some money and run to the store and grab some condoms and douches." Tasha was in the room right next to Halleigh's.

"No problem." Halleigh smiled at the thought of a day off. She hung up the phone and went over to finish her coke before leaving for the store, glad to play the role of errand girl over whore any day.

Scratch, the neighborhood crackhead, sat in the alley next to a store, the place he had called home for the past two weeks after losing his bed at the homeless shelter. His body was yearning for another fix of crack, heroin, something. He'd been without a shot since earlier that day, and now here it was nighttime and it was like he was turning into a werewolf. His body throbbed as he clenched his stomach tightly. He frantically scratched his itchy and irritated arms, which felt like something was trying to burst up out of his skin. He stood up. His legs were as weak as a boxer's in the twelfth round who had taken some hard punches. He had to try and think of a way he could get some money for his next fix. Scratch walked out of the alley, where the streetlights illuminated the sidewalk.

In his forty-one years, he had been through hell and back, and his near death appearance showed it. He had once been Flint's "push man," but now he was nothing more than a junkie. In the late eighties, he'd tried a dose of his own supply, and ever since then, he had been on the opposite side of the game, hooked on heroin and crack cocaine. Karma wasn't no joke.

Scratch paced back and forth in front of the store, desperately seeking a way to get right.

"Ay, brotha," he said to a man walking out of the store. "Look out for Scratch. Spare me a dollar, young blood."

The man ignored him and proceeded to his car.

"Come on, man," Scratch continued to plead, legs wobbling, "I know you got it. I know you got some change back up in there."

The man got into his car, shaking his head in disgust.

Scratch wanted to fire off a string of curse words at the man, but a pain shot through Scratch's stomach as his body went through withdrawal. The only thing that came out of his mouth was a sigh of pain. Once the pain began to let up, Scratch slowly eased up back into standing position. Still clenching his stomach, he saw a beautiful girl in high heels and a miniskirt walking by him toward the store. "Ay, baby girl, can you spare a dolla? Come on, baby girl. Hook Scratch up."

The bell over the door rang as the girl, her head hung low, walked right past him and entered the store without paying him a bit of mind. And it wasn't as if she was trying to ignore him like the man before her had so blatantly done. It was just that she was so consumed with her own personal thoughts that she hadn't heard a word Scratch had said to her.

Scratch watched through the store's glass door

as the girl stood in line at the counter, dug into her bra, and pulled out wrinkled bills. His mind began to work overtime. "Bingo!" he whispered. He now had a plan.

Chapter Three

Halleigh had just walked down the street and into the corner store, still high from the line she had inhaled minutes earlier. High as a kite, she kept her head down as she picked up a few items and then stood in line.

As she had aimlessly strolled to the store, her thoughts, just as they always managed to do, suddenly landed on Malek. Now she stood in the line, still consumed by thoughts of her past boyfriend, whom she thought was going to be her future.

I miss that boy so much. I wonder if he ever thinks about me. Halleigh's eyes watered as Malek's mother's words filled her head, reminding her that there was probably no way on earth Malek was thinking about her.

"Halleigh, I'm sorry to be the one to break this to you, but Malek left this morning. His father came into town and thought that it would be good for him if he got away

from all this madness, until things could die down and get cleared up. He didn't want to see you, honey."

Halleigh caught a tear that had managed to escape her eye and wiped it away. She couldn't believe Malek had just up and left her just like that. Her mind understood the words Mrs. Johnson had spoken, but her heart just couldn't believe them.

Ironically, Mrs. Johnson couldn't believe she was telling Halleigh that boldfaced lie either, but she had to do something to keep Halleigh, whom she always felt was no good for her son, away from him. So, after filling Halleigh's head with all those lies about Malek abandoning her and not wanting to see her, Mrs. Johnson had simply repented, making the excuse to God that she had done it for the sake of her son.

Lost in her thoughts, Halleigh didn't even notice the crackhead eyeballing her through the glass door from outside the store. In all actuality, she'd never even noticed him when he tried to bum money from her as she was entering the store. But she would certainly notice him in a few minutes.

Scratch searched frantically throughout the alley. He needed to find some sort of weapon so that he could rob the girl he'd been scoping out inside the store. He felt bad about what he planned to do, but he had to get the monkey off his back, and quick. At the time, the dead presidents she kept stashed in her brasierre seemed like his only option right now. And since opportunity was knocking, he'd be a fool not to answer the door.

He grabbed a short but thick stick off the ground and quickly put it up under his shirt. He then proceeded to arrange it so that it poked through his shirt to look like a gun. He leaned against the side of the building in the alley and awaited his prey.

"Give me yo' mu'fuckin' money!" he whispered, trying to practice his approach. For years he had managed to get high without ever having to knock an old lady upside the head; ironically, something he was proud of. The girl he was preparing to rob wasn't no old lady, but still, he was doing something he thought he'd never have to do and he felt ashamed. As an addict, Scratch had always comforted himself with the logic that he wasn't hurting anybody but himself by getting high. But now that was about to change.

He looked down at the stick and knew that it wouldn't pass as a gun. "Damn! This shit ain't gon' work," he said to himself. He threw the stick down in frustration and became agitated as he sought out another weapon in the litter-filled alley.

Scratch's eyes focused on a broken beer bottle. "Yeah, that right there will do it." He walked over and picked up the bottle. He then rehearsed his line again. "Give me yo' mu'fuckin' money!" he spat softly. "Or I'll cut your fuckin' throat." Scratch smiled, figuring he had found the right approach, but then his smile quickly faded. "What if she tries to run?" Scratch looked down at his wobbling legs and knew that he wasn't up for a chase. "Damn," he said, throwing down the broken bottle.

Scratch knew that the girl would be walking out of the store any minute. He had to think quickly.

He looked down at his feet and then got an idea. He took off his worn-out shoe and then pulled off his soiled, stinky sock. He gathered up a bunch of rocks from the ground and filled the sock with them. He held up the sock, and the most horrendous odor reeked off of it.

"Well, goddamn!" He grimaced as the foul odor invaded his nose. "Whew! If the rocks won't knock her out, the smell sho' in the hell will," he said, quickly distancing the sock from his face.

Once again, he leaned up against the wall and practiced his approach, which seemed even less threatening with a sock. "Fuck!" He knew that the "sock and rock" method wouldn't scare anybody and decided to resort back to using the stick as a fake gun. He shuffled around real quick and found the stick that he'd discarded earlier. But that's when he noticed an even bigger one. "Just in case I do have to knock her ass out," he told himself. He threw down the smaller one and took the bigger stick and placed it underneath his shirt, as if he had a burner. "Yeah." He shook his head, finally satisfied with his choice. "That's what Scratch talking about."

At that moment, Scratch heard the doorbell jingle, signaling that his would-be victim was exiting the store. Then he heard the clicking of the girl's high-heeled shoes. Just as he had anticipated, the girl came strutting out with a bag in her hand. He quickly ducked and leaned into the alley and waited for her to pass so he could grab her. However, his guilty conscience began to set in. And in just those few seconds while he waited for her to cross his path, he went back and forth with himself about going through with his plan.

But the little red devil with the pitchfork sitting on his left shoulder got the better of him. When he saw the girl walk past, he went for it. He quickly grabbed her from the back and placed his hands over her mouth, dragging her into the alley and slamming her against the wall. "Give me all yo' money!" Scratch was shaking just as much as the girl was.

"Please don't hurt me!" she screamed, dropping the items in her hands, then raising her arms in surrender.

Scratch pushed her against the wall and pointed his fake gun at her. "Give me yo' cash and you won't get hurt," he whispered harshly.

"Please don't kill me," she said, her knees shaking uncontrollably. One would think she was going through withdrawal as well.

"Just give me all the dough and I won't shoot."

Just as Scratch had watched her do before, she anxiously went into her bra to pull out all the money she had. Scratch looked into the young girl's eyes and thought she looked familiar. As he stared into her eyes a little longer, he frowned. "Halleigh?" he whispered, lowering his fake gun.

Afraid to say anything, she nodded her head, not wanting to give him a reason to pop off.

"You Sharina's daughter, ain't you?" Scratch asked. He knew Halleigh's face well, because of Sharina. The two looked more like sisters than mother and daughter, and he knew that since it wasn't Sharina, it had to be her baby girl.

"Well, I'll be damned," Scratch said as he smiled. "I can't believe I'm standing here looking dead at Sharina's baby girl."

Sharina had been one of Scratch's get-high buddies, and he'd seen pictures of Halleigh over at Sharina's house whenever he was over there getting high. He had even seen Halleigh in person a couple of times, but of course she never paid her mother's dope partners any mind.

Halleigh nodded her head again, confirming that in fact she was Sharina's daughter. A small glimmer of hope ran through her. Since he knew her mother, maybe he really wouldn't hurt her. For the first time since Halleigh could remember, she had never been more glad to be her Sharina's daughter. She knew it had to come in handy and do her some good at one point in her life, and what better time than now?

"Can you let me go?" Halleigh asked Scratch, her back still pressed against the wall.

Scratch looked down and forgot about the fake gun. "Oh yeah," he said. He pulled the stick out from under his shirt and then threw it to the ground.

"You out here robbing people with sticks?" Halleigh asked, a sense of relief passing through her. She couldn't help but chuckle, although what she really wanted to do was take that stick and crack him upside the head; not for trying to rob her with it, but just for the pure stupidity of him thinking he could rob anybody with it.

"It almost worked, didn't it?" Scratched let out a slight chuckle himself. "What is a girl like you doing out here on these mean streets this time of night anyway?" Sudden concern now seemed to take over Scratch's mind.

The last thing Halleigh wanted to do was stand out there and have a conversation with a man who'd just tried to rob her. She wanted to leave the raggedy man in the alley, but she knew he had a jones. She could tell, because she'd seen the same look in her mother's eyes many a night. And with that, thoughts of her mother and this man's relationship piqued her curiosity.

"I was just running to the store," Halleigh told the man. "How do you know my mother?"

"Me and Sharina used to get high together." Scratch thought back to the days when he and Sharina used to do more than just get high together. Back before Scratch was so strung out, he and Sharina used to kick it. Back then, neither one of them were users. He remembered how Sharina used to look up to him for being such a major player in the game. But once she learned of his drug use, she looked at him the same way a sinner would look at her pastor who done fell from grace. She felt like, hell, if Scratch could do it, then why couldn't she?

Scratch tried to tell Sharina that the shit wasn't for her; but who was he to tell her that when, by then, he had started using pretty heavy himself? Still looking up to him, Sharina wanted to be on that same high. And before they knew it, the two found themselves no longer hooking up to keep each other company, but hooking up to get high together.

"How's Sharina doing these days?" Scratch asked, thinking about their pre-addict times together.

"I don't know. I don't fuck with her like that no more." Bitterness laced Halleigh's tone. "Last time I saw her she was more worried about a fix than she was me."

Scratch could sense Halleigh's feeling of disgust toward her mother and made an attempt to comfort her. "Aaah, that's just Sharina. But you know what? High or not, she sure did love her some you." Scratch smiled. "She loved her baby girl; talked about you all the time." Scratch wasn't exaggerating. Sharina did love her daughter with all of her heart, and she still did to this day. It's just that her mind had power over her heart; and her mind needed the drug.

"Oh yeah," Halleigh spat. "Well, actions speak louder than words."

"Look, you don't understand, baby girl. That crack rock ain't no joke. Scratch know that shit. It ain't just no little monkey either. It's more like a gorilla; like King Kong, you know. It overpowers everything. So don't be too hard on your moms."

"Tuh, that's an understatement." Halleigh begged to differ.

Scratch could see that he wasn't going to get anywhere with the subject of Halleigh and her mother, so he switched it back to himself. "Anyway, speaking of that monkey-gorilla thing . . ." Scratch turned on his smooth, convincing tone. "Why don't you hook Scratch up, Li'l Rina?" Scratch begged. "Let me hold something so I can get right."

Halleigh was about to walk away and leave him there, but the fact that he knew her mother softened her up a bit. As much as she wanted every vein in her body to pump nothing but pure hatred for her mother, there was just a little part of her that still loved Sharina. At the same time, though, Halleigh was still a little scared of what Scratch might try to put himself up to next. Having witnessed firsthand what a person was willing to do for a hit, she wouldn't be surprised if he'd try something even worse. Yeah, he'd spared her, but what about the next person?

Halleigh looked down at her money, and before she handed some to Scratch, she asked, "What do you get from getting high off of crack? I never understood why my mother did it." Halleigh never even considered that using cocaine really wasn't any better than using crack. She didn't see herself as being anything like the dope fiends she'd encountered. Getting high wasn't something she felt she needed to do. It was something she just *wanted* to do.

"So much fucked-up shit has happened to me in my life, Li'l Rina. It's like when you're high, all that goes away."

Halleigh could feel that. She knew exactly what Scratch was speaking about. Halleigh peeled a twenty-dollar bill from her stack of money and handed it to Scratch. Then she began to walk away. Suddenly, she stopped in her tracks and turned around. "What did you say your name was again?"

Scratch's eyes lit up as he gazed at the money, knowing that he could finally get the monkey off his back. He looked up at Halleigh with his gap-toothed smile. "Scratch. Everybody knows me as Scratch."

"Well, Scratch, don't get yourself killed out here

robbing people with sticks," Halleigh said with a slight grin.

"You betta count yo' blessings, baby girl. A stick is the least of your worries. I was going to unleash my stanking-ass sock on you with the ol' 'sock and rock,' " Scratch said jokingly. He looked down at his one bare foot. He hadn't had time to put his sock and shoe back on.

Halleigh grinned and started walking away.

"If you ever need to talk, come and holla at me, good ol' Scratch. The rest of me might not be right, but I got good ears for listening. I'll be right here," Scratch yelled as he watched Halleigh walk away into the darkness.

Chapter Four

Halleigh leaned back on her bed and closed her eyes. She was tired, and her body felt extremely drained. She had swooped her shoulder-length hair, which she usually wore flat-ironed straight with feathered side bangs, into a ponytail. The fairly new blonde highlights complemented her light skin.

Halleigh was cute, but she never saw herself as beautiful, or anything close to it, especially when she was next to her former high school best friend, Nikki. Nikki had been her only friend, besides Malek. Nikki's mom had got on that stuff too, which gave both Halleigh and Nikki a common ground to stand on. Halleigh hadn't seen Nikki in more than a year, and although every now and then she thought about kickin' it with her old friend, on the flip side, Halleigh was glad of it. It wasn't because she didn't miss her friend or want to see her, but she didn't want her friend to see her now.

Turning over to look at the clock, Halleigh saw that it read 8:00 P.M. She let out a loud sigh, knowing that she was supposed to be over at the hotel at 11:30 P.M. *I just want to get some rest before then,* she thought as she balled up on the bed, put the pillow on top of her head, and turned to face the wall. The only thing that she could think of was the comfortable sleep that she was drifting into.

Less than five minutes after Halleigh closed her eyes, Mimi came bursting into the room and sat down on the bed. "Hal, you awake?" Mimi whispered, gently nudging her. "Hal, you up?" She ran her hands down her braided hair extensions, which she wore straight back, with baby hair surrounding the edges, the braids falling right above her butt.

Halleigh heard Mimi, but she tried to ignore her in hopes that she would let her get some sleep.

"Halleigh, wake up, girl. I need a favor."

Halleigh sighed loudly and removed the pillow from her eyes. She looked up at the girl she once saw as her savior. Halleigh met Mimi the day Malek had gone to jail for the robbery. Halleigh was camping out at the police station, waiting for Malek to be arraigned, whenever that was going to be. She had no idea how long she would have to wait there, but she had no other place to go. She couldn't go home. Her mother had just allowed two dope boys to rape her as a trade for the dope she had stolen from them. Sharina sat in her room getting high while her daughter's virginity, the virginity she'd promised to give to Malek that very night, was taken from her.

The fact that she didn't have anyplace to go was the reason Malek was committing the robbery in the first place. He was only trying to get money for her to pay for a hotel, at least for that night, until they could figure out something to do. But once Malek was apprehended and taken to jail, Halleigh still ended up with no place to go. Malek had promised to be there for her, so she returned the promise by being there for him, even if it meant spending hours upon hours in the lobby of the police station. But not even that was a solution when Halleigh was kicked out of the police station for loitering.

It was out in the rain, on the streets of Flint, when Mimi befriended Halleigh. Mimi had just been released by the police after being arrested on a prostitution charge.

"I'm Mimi. You can crash at my spot if you need to, at least for the night. My daddy will probably be able to help you out too. He can help you get your boy out of jail if you want him to."

Halleigh didn't know Mimi from the man on the moon, and had seen her for the first time when she was inside cursing out the police officers as they released her from handcuffs. Out of options and figuring that anything would be better than being on the streets, she accepted Mimi's offer.

"You sure your daddy won't mind?" Halleigh asked.

Mimi smirked and looked Halleigh up and down and then licked her lips. "Nah, he won't mind. Trust me."

Mimi continued to shake Halleigh. "You up?" Mimi repeated once again.

"I am now," Halleigh snapped. "Damn, girl, that sleep was feeling good. What you want?"

"I need a favor." Mimi stopped and waited to see Halleigh's reaction.

Halleigh looked at her as if to say, *And?*

Mimi continued, "I got this private party lined up. It pays one thousand dollars for each girl."

Halleigh could see the dollar signs forming in Mimi's greedy eyes. Once the idea of getting some paper set in, Mimi was unstoppable. Nothing came between her and her paper. Halleigh had often wondered why Manolo had chosen Tasha to be the madam versus Mimi, who stayed on the paper chase and made sure her money was right. Then again, Halleigh surmised, with that much paper flowing through Mimi's hands, she was too stuck on herself to be that damn loyal to the game. And it wasn't no secret amongst the girls that Mimi was forever trying to hook up gigs that paid her behind Manolo's back.

"They want two girls for just a couple of hours."

"When?" Halleigh asked hesitantly.

Mimi then delivered the catch. "Tonight."

"Oh, hell nah," Halleigh replied quickly, shaking her head from side to side.

"Come on, Hal, please. You know I can't miss this money," Mimi pleaded. "I'd do it for you."

"Like hell you would." Halleigh rolled her eyes.

Halleigh thought about that time Manolo wanted Mimi to do the unthinkable as far as a hooker was concerned: fuck for free. Mimi refused to have

Manolo's back on that one. And in return, Mimi had gotten beat down by Manolo for not turning that trick he'd instructed her to turn with some baldhead, crooked cop named Troy. Granted, Troy wasn't paying no thousand dollars or anything near it. As a matter of fact, he wasn't paying anything. Manolo just wanted to have a cop in his pocket, but Mimi didn't recognize that and refused to give up the pussy for free. She later regretted her disobedience.

So Halleigh knew better than to fall for Mimi's "I'd-do-it-for-you" look of pity. And on top of that, Halleigh was almost certain that Manolo knew nothing about this little private party. Mimi was always doing side jobs that Manolo didn't know about. She kept a tight leash on her regulars just for that simple fact. Mimi had her game set up so tight that she'd schooled her loyal regulars to call up Tasha and request one thing: something simple like a blow job. Once the john showed up in her hotel room, she'd have him pay her directly for the service that he really wanted.

To date, none of Mimi's little schemes had ever backfired on her, but when it did, the last thing Halleigh wanted to do was to be there, caught up in the midst of it all. Halleigh knew just as well as Mimi did that if Manolo ever found out, there'd be hell to pay.

"No, fuck that, Mimi. I know you ain't forgotten that ass-whupping Manolo put on you at Wild Thangs," Halleigh said, trying to jog Mimi's memory of the beat-down at the strip club Manolo and Sweets, his superior, ran.

Mimi got this salty look on her face after Halleigh's smart remark. Hell yeah, she remembered being beaten nearly unconscious and she thought that Halleigh was trying to be a smart ass by throwing it back in her face. But all Halleigh was really doing was trying to make sure that Manolo hadn't knocked her upside her head so hard that she had lost her mind. After all, Halleigh figured Mimi had to have lost her mind in order to keep trying to do her own thing on the side; cutting Manolo out completely.

Although Mimi wanted to remind Halleigh about the ass-whippin' she too had endured at the hands of Manolo, she decided not to start a verbal war with the person whose help she needed so desperately right about now.

"Please, Hal, you know I wouldn't even be asking you to do this if I didn't need you there." Mimi used the most sincere tone she could muster up to try to convince her fellow comrade to help her out.

Halleigh stayed strong. "Uh-uh. Nope." She shook her head adamantly. "You better ask Keesha or somebody. You ain't about to pull me into no bullshit." Halleigh knew that if anybody else was out to make paper like Mimi, it was Keesha. That's why it was the first name that had popped into Halleigh's head. She felt sure if presented with the opportunity, Keesha would do it, and therefore Halleigh would be off the hook.

Keesha, who worked at Wild Thangs as a waitress, had been wanting to be a Manolo Mami, as Manolo's hoes were referred to, since forever. Manolo had ten girls working for him, including Tasha, who didn't have to turn tricks because she held madam status.

Working the gig with Mimi would have definitely made Keesha feel like one of the girls, but Mimi didn't trust Keesha as far as she could throw her.

Mimi stood up, trying to convince Halleigh to roll with her. "Come on, now. Girl, you know I can't get Keesha to do it with me. That snitching-ass bitch, she can't hold water. She'd be the first one running to tell Manolo, to try to get a bitch in trouble so that she can take my place. You know I can't trust her ass." Mimi cuddled next to Halleigh and brushed her hair with the back of her hand. "You know you my girl. I need you there. Come on, Halleigh. Just have my back this one time," Mimi begged.

Halleigh sighed in frustration. *I know if I don't roll with her, she gon' do it anyway. I can't let her go solo.* Halleigh knew that Mimi wouldn't let a dollar slip through her fingers. With or without her, she was going. And if the girls had learned anything, it was to be paired up when hustling.

A few years ago, one of the dancers at Wild Thangs left with a customer who wanted to do a little more than stick money down her thong. The customer had been buying the girl twenty-dollar drinks all night long. He was dressed in a suit and just appeared to be paid.

The customer ended up taking her back to his condo, where two more of his dudes were waiting for her. All three men ended up having their way with her for the next four hours. They paid her money, throwing it to her afterwards as if she were less than human. All the things they had her doing, she did out of complete fear because they were so drunk and high and dominating that she was afraid what might happen to her if she refused. But it went without saying that no amount of money was worth it.

After that incident, Tasha set a house rule that the girls had to work in pairs if they were going to turn tricks outside of the club or hotel atmosphere. And even though Mimi's hustle wasn't one of Manolo's assignments, Halleigh knew she still had to be there for Mimi.

"All right, girl . . . damn, I'll do it." Halleigh sighed. "You know you get on my nerves, don't you?" Halleigh sat up in the bed, surrendering to Mimi's pleas.

"Thank you, thank you, thank you," Mimi whispered eagerly as she hugged Halleigh and then got up from the bed. She pulled out a tube of lip gloss and began coating her lips as if she were preparing on the spot.

"Who are these niggas anyway?" Halleigh inquired.

"Jamaica Joe and his people," Mimi said under her breath. She turned toward the full-length mirror and applied another coat of lip gloss.

"Jamaica Joe and his people?" Halleigh abruptly got up out of the bed, realizing that this was, in fact, the actual catch. "Hell no, Mimi! Are you out of your mind? Jamaica Joe?" Halleigh began pacing. "Manolo will kill both of us. You know Sweets and Manolo don't fuck with them North Side niggas. And what if Joe finds out we down with Manolo? That nigga might pop off just because. He might try to use us as ransom or something. I'm sorry, Mimi, but you are on your own with this one."

"Come on, Hal. You already said yes," Mimi reminded her.

"But that's before I knew who the dudes that hired us were." Halleigh couldn't believe that Mimi still expected her to lend a helping hand after dropping Jamaica Joe's name. Hell, she couldn't believe Mimi had even given it a second thought. Maybe Manolo had hit her upside her head to hard, because she had definitely lost her marbles. "You done lost your mind. Manolo will have our heads on a platter and you know it."

Halleigh wasn't saying anything that Mimi hadn't already thought of. She was well aware of the beef between Sweets and Joe. Manolo was down with Sweets, who was Joe's archenemy, and this scenario was nothing but trouble. If Sweets ever found out that Manolo's girls were associated with Joe in any kind of way, then he would make Manolo teach them a lesson they wouldn't soon forget.

But Mimi was a risk-taker. At the end of the day, she knew that together, they made too much money for Manolo to ever get rid of them, or to hurt them bad enough that they couldn't eventually make him more money.

"Please, Halleigh? Look, it'll be short and quick. We can be in and out of there in an hour. One hour and we'll be a thousand dollars richer, and you ain't even gon' have to split that shit." Of course, when dealing with Mimi, she always had a scheme inside of her original scheme.

Jamaica Joe was actually paying $1,500 per girl. He knew that in order to get Mimi to take such a risk and fuck with him, he'd have to be willing to pay the price. But he didn't mind at all. He got a thrill knowing that he had the power to get a couple of his rival team's cheerleaders to come cheer for his team for a little while. And even though he was willing to pay each girl $1,500, Mimi decided, that she was entitled to a $500 finder's fee. This was a $2,000 come-up for her. She needed Halleigh to come through for her.

The more Halleigh thought about it, the more she realized that she, too, could use that money. Working for Manolo, she barely made enough money to take care of her personal needs. The split with Manolo was 80/20, Manolo receiving the larger share, of course. He felt as though the girls required less since he was the one who had to keep the roof over their heads; since he was the one who provided their clothes and food. Halleigh knew that if she went with Mimi on this little one-hour gig, she could pocket the money without Manolo getting a cut.

"All right, I'll go. One hour and then I'm out," Halleigh said matter-of-factly.

"One hour, I promise!" Mimi exclaimed with excitement, running over and hugging and kissing Halleigh on the cheek. "We'll drop by the party at around ten o'clock. We're not set to go on until eleven-thirty, so that gives us an hour to do what we got to do and a half hour to check in with Tasha so that she won't know what's up."

"Where are we going to tell Tasha that we are

at?" Halleigh asked, making sure that Mimi had crossed all the Ts and dotted all the Is.

"I don't know . . . we'll just tell her a john wanted a private at his house or something and that we paired up for safety. I'll check in the money for a blow job or something out of my share. Don't worry, Hal. Your girl's got this."

"You better know what you're doing." Halleigh walked by Mimi and lightly swatted her on the ass as she headed to the shower to get ready.

"Oh, I know what I'm doing all right," Mimi was talking to herself because Halleigh had already left the room. She rubbed her hands together in greed. "I'm about to get paid is what I'm doing." Mimi tapped herself on the shoulder for a job well done in getting Halleigh to roll with her. Next, she said a small prayer. "Lord, please get us through this night without anything going wrong." Mimi then left the room, not realizing that tonight, she'd need more than just a prayer to get her out of the situation she had gotten herself, and now Halleigh, into. She'd need a miracle.

Chapter Five

Tariq maneuvered the '99 Chevy Suburban into the Valley, one of Flint's South Side neighborhoods. His windows were tinted, so he didn't have to worry about anyone seeing his face. But he was still nervous about being out of his own territory.

This nigga bullshitting, having me meet him on the South, Tariq thought. *I done murked too many niggas on this side of town to be riding around this bitch solo.* Tariq kept checking his rearview mirror to make sure no one was tailing him. The last thing he was trying to do was to get caught slipping. He put his hand on the snub-nosed pistol tucked at his waistline for reassurance. *This is all the back-up I need.* He bobbed his head to Tupac's "Me and My Girlfriend."

Tariq turned onto Tebo Street and parked his truck on the curb in front of the small blue-and-white house. He turned off the ignition and sat nervously inside the car for a couple of minutes. He had to get his head right, to make sure that he was prepared to do what he was about to do; because one thing he knew for sure was that once he stepped foot out of that car and went up to that house, there would be no turning back.

He looked around cautiously before he unlocked his car door and stepped out. He kept his hand on his pistol the entire time as he walked swiftly up the driveway and knocked on the back door.

Tap, tap, tap!

He knocked on the steel screen door. A few seconds passed, but it felt like hours as Tariq continuously looked over his shoulders. *This mu'fucka better come on,* he thought, stepping nervously from side to side.

Tariq knocked a little more forcefully this time.

Sweets finally appeared at the door. "Fuck you beating down my door for, nigga?" He was shirtless and wore only jean shorts and Nike flip-flops. His tattooed, hardcore body was ripped like LL Cool J's. It was a body most women would die for, and some men, too, considering Sweets was a "homo thug" who slept with both men and women.

"Man, you gon' let me in or what?" Tariq looked around, still observing his surroundings.

Sweets smiled coyly and replied "Oh yeah, I forgot. You scared of us South Side niggas. Only time y'all North Siders got heart is when you cliqued up."

"Just open the door," Tariq responded impatiently.

Sweets opened the door and stepped to the side as Tariq walked into his house. "We in the basement," he said and began to walk down the stairs.

"Who the fuck is *we*?" Tariq asked. "I don't need more than your ears hearing what I got to say, nah mean?"

"Nah, don't worry about it. I understand what's up. My man down here ain't a street nigga. He ain't worried 'bout what you talking."

Tariq reluctantly walked down the steps behind Sweets, patting his weapon for reassurance just in case something did jump off.

The basement was arranged more like a den, with a sofa, love seat, and a 72-inch plasma TV all positioned comfortably in the small space. Sweets took a seat on the sofa. His company, who was a dark-skinned dude with a striped button-up shirt on, snuggled up against him.

Tariq almost gagged at the sight. *This gay mu'-fucka,* he thought, turning his nose up. Tariq was disgusted, not only because of the sight before him, but because it reminded him of how his own pops was living.

Tariq's mom thought she was the luckiest woman in the world when Tariq Sr. chose to make a home with her. Although the two never married, they were together for ten years total. When Tariq was eight years old, his pops left him and his mom. Tariq never knew what happened. He just came home from school one day to find all of his father's things gone. When he asked his mother where his father was, her only reply was, "He's left."

Until Tariq was about twelve years old, he hated

his father for abandoning them. He wondered how he could just pick up and leave without even saying good-bye. Tariq would spend hours in his room alone, blaming himself for his father up and leaving. His relationship with his mother, which had once been closeknit and healthy, became severed and weak. Thinking that it might help pull Tariq out of his slumping funk of depression, his mother decided it might be a good ideal to tell Tariq the truth about his father. She decided to do it before it was too late for them to even be able to mend their own mother and son relationship.

The day Tariq's mother sat him down and told him that his father didn't just up and leave, but that she had put him out and ordered him to never come around them again, Tariq immediately shifted his hate from his father to his mother. He couldn't imagine why she would do such a thing. He began to disrespect her by cursing and yelling. It was then she knew that she had to tell him the full reason why she had done so.

Tariq's mother explained to him that his father had used her; had used both of them to paint an image in order to cover up who he really was. While on the outside he looked like the typical husband and father, on the inside, he truly desired men. Convinced that some homosexual spirit was on him, she put him out and told him that if he ever came around her or her son, she would expose him for who he really was. Tariq's father wasn't willing to come out of the closet and face the prejudice of society and his family and friends, from whom he had managed for so many years to keep the truth.

So he agreed, packing up all of his things and leaving, knowing he'd never be able to see his son again. Within months of leaving Tariq and his mother, he found another woman whom he impregnated. She gave him another child, behind whom he hid his true self.

Upon hearing that his father was homosexual, the only thing that came to Tariq's mind was how people would always tell him how he was just like his father, how he looked just like his father and how when he grew up, he was probably going to be just like his father. This made Tariq sick to his stomach. After hearing the bomb his mother had dropped on him, the last person he wanted to be like was his dad.

From that point on, Tariq felt he had to do everything possible to prove himself as a real man, and not some soft-ass punk buried in a man's body like his father. So he took to acting out; acting hard and getting into trouble. He hooked up with the hardest cats in school to prove he wasn't a sissy. He went through girls one after another to prove that he liked girls and not men. The night he raped Halleigh, it was just another way of proving his manhood; having control and power over someone else.

His father's lifestyle had messed up his head in more ways than one, and now seeing Sweets hugged with another man so openly made him want to vomit.

Sweets picked up an Xbox controller and resumed the Madden game he'd been playing with his manfriend before Tariq arrived. "What you got for me?" Sweets asked as his friend licked his neck teasingly.

Tariq looked at Sweets in disbelief. "Yo, man, can we handle this in private?" Tariq didn't mask the irritation in his voice.

Sweets whispered in his companion's ear, and then the dude rose from the couch, mean-mugging Tariq, smacking his lips and rolling his eyes before leaving the room.

Tariq just shook his head and waited until the man left the room. One thing he could say about Sweets, though; he definitely wasn't on the down low. He kept his shit wide and out in the open. But his reputation and credential on the street let cats know that in spite of what things looked like, he was a real nigga when it came to handling his business.

"What you got for me?"

"What you got for me?" Tariq asked right back. He was about to give Sweets some valuable information, but it wouldn't come without a price. Hell, nothing in this world came for free.

"It depends on what you tell me," Sweets replied. "I'm trying to murder this nigga. He hit my li'l man, Rah-Rah, at the Berston Park shootout last year. It's about time we got back at him, you know. Can't let that shit rest . . . no, no," Sweets stated to himself more than to Tariq.

Certain members of Sweets' crew had been wanting to retaliate right after the shooting. Sweets knew how the game worked, though. He knew that Jamaica Joe and his crew would be expecting immediate retaliation and would certainly have their guards up. He felt that it would be better to wait it out and catch them fools off guard, and with the help of Tariq, it looked as though they were about to do just that.

A streak of guilt ran through Tariq as he thought about exactly what it was he was planning to do to his comrade. But then he thought about how his comrade had been so quick to put the young boy Malek on. *This nigga been acting like Malek is his right hand instead of me, the nigga that done had his back for all these years. That li'l nigga ain't put in no work, but Joe got this dude in the cut like he belongs.*

"Joe having a get-together tonight at his crib on Coldwater," Tariq began to sing.

Sweets didn't take his eyes off the game he was playing when he said, "What I'm supposed to do with that information, fam?"

"I'm just letting you know there's a window of opportunity, if you trying to take it."

"Yo' mama ain't never teach you not to take your fight to your enemy's house? Ain't no telling what he got in that mu'fucka," Sweets stated. "What they looking like anyway, as far as heat is concerned? They gon' have the burners on 'em?"

"That's just it," Tariq said in a tone that told Sweets if he'd just shut up and let him finish, he'd have all his questions answered. "Ain't nobody allowed to take no heat in Joe's house. Niggas be leaving them shits in their whips. Joe gon' be the only one holding."

"I don't know," Sweets replied, shaking his head as he operated the remote control. "This might not be too valuable. Sounds kind of risky to me."

Tariq felt that Sweets might be trying to play him by pretending that the information was of little use, so that he didn't have to pay Tariq for it. But Tariq knew Sweets would still use the info, so he decided to throw in a little extra incentive, just to make sure that Sweets sealed the deal. "I know where the bricks at too. I can put you up on them, if the split is right."

Sweets paused the game system. "The bricks in his house?" he asked. He had now given Tariq his full, undivided attention.

Tariq nodded. "In the basement. Fifteen joints in the safe. You get in, hit Joe, and then take the bricks."

All of this sounded too good to be true, so he had to question Tariq's intentions. "What you getting out of all this?" Sweets asked suspiciously.

Tariq knew that he better pick his words carefully. He didn't want Sweets to think that he was trying to play both sides of the fence. "It's time for a new era, baby. I ain't making that much paper under Joe. He put this new kid on, and it seems to me that the li'l nigga making more moves than me. So, to make a long story short, it's time to take what I'm owed."

Sweets thought for a minute. Tariq was the type he feared most on his own team: a jealous nigga. He knew how they operated. Their loyalty was only as good as the dough coming their way that paid for their loyalty. And now that it seemed that another nigga was cutting into Tariq's paper, he was ready to turn against the captain. It always added salt to the wound when the next player in line was some young cat who still had milk behind his ears.

"You mean that kid Malek? Is that who you feel is steppin' on your toes?" Sweets had been hearing about Malek on the streets. The kid was definitely coming up in the game.

"Yeah."

"Yeah, I been hearing 'bout the little nigga. Used to hoop, right? My li'l nigga shot up his ol' miss a while back. He stopped one of my soldiers from hitting Joe at Berston. That was the only time we had a chance to get him, too," Sweets said, regretting that his crew missed Joe that time.

Tariq was surprised to hear that the Shottah Boyz were responsible for killing Malek's mother, and obviously his stepfather too. The shooters had been unknown to him until that moment. Even though Jamaica Joe had put money on the table for anyone who brought back information on the shooting, nothing had surfaced.

Tariq quickly got back on task and cut to the chase. "This is your chance to get Joe, fam. It might not be another chance. He doesn't put down his guard a lot," Tariq said, getting frustrated.

Sweets nodded his head in understanding. He reached under his sofa and pulled out a roll of money: five thousand dollars, to be exact. Tossing it to Tariq, he asked, "So what time should I crash the party?"

Tariq flipped through the rolls and then replied, "Party start at eleven o'clock. Joe lives on Coldwater, between Jennings and Clio, not that spot over there on Harriet Street where everybody think he lays his head. Come through around midnight. I'll make sure that I'm at the door by then, and I'll let you slide through."

"You do that," Sweets told him, nodding his head because he knew it was on. Revenge was finally about to be served.

Chapter Six

Halleigh looked around nervously as she and Mimi walked up the long circular driveway to Jamaica Joe's luxury house. It was a sand-colored, five-level stucco house with a brick front. There were no flowers or anything like that planted, but the landscape was immaculate. All of the bushes were evenly trimmed, surrounded by black mulch. The house had to be around 4,500 square feet, not including the attached three-car garage.

"Damn," Mimi said, admiring the mini-castle. "Shit, I should have charged they asses two grand each." She looked around. "After all, what's another five hundred each to this nigga?"

"You mean a thousand each," Halleigh corrected her.

Mimi thought for a moment, realizing that she almost blew her cover by revealing the fact that Joe was really paying $1,500 per girl instead of the

$1,000 she had told Halleigh he was paying. "Oh yeah, that's right, girl. You know I'm not good at math."

"Not when it comes to other people's money you're not," Halleigh said sarcastically. "But I will agree that from the looks of this house," Halleigh stated as she too admired the dwelling, "they could have afforded it, that's for sure."

The two women made their way to the back door, which Mimi had been instructed by Joe to use. When they got there, the only thing that stood between them and the man on the other side was a glass storm door.

"Y'all the dancers?" the man asked, opening the door for them.

"Naw, we here to deliver pizza," Mimi said sarcastically as she made her way past the man. Halleigh followed close behind.

Instantly the women's nostrils were filled with the smell of weed as they peeped out their surroundings. Mimi appeared to be confident that the gig would go down without a hitch and that Manolo would never find out about it. After all, no one who associated with the North Side crews associated with the South Side crews, so she knew that there was no mutual player to go back and run his mouth. Halleigh, on the other hand, wasn't as convinced as Mimi that Manolo would never find out. She couldn't stop the butterflies from fluttering in her stomach.

"Mimi, are you sure about this?"

"Yeah. Just chill, Hal." Mimi spotted Joe standing at the bottom of the basement steps. "There's Joe right there."

Joe ascended the steps and hugged Mimi as if they were old friends.

Halleigh took a deep breath to calm her nerves. *One hour and then we're out,* she reminded herself. Now that she stood there, she couldn't believe that she had let Mimi talk her into this madness.

"Joe, this is my girl, Sunshine," Mimi said, using the name Manolo had branded Halleigh with. "But you can call her Sunny." Mimi turned to Halleigh. "Sunny, this is Joe."

Joe nodded a "what up" at Halleigh and then stepped out of the landing and up onto the main level of his luxurious home. Mimi grabbed Halleigh's hand, and they followed Joe toward the back of the house, where the bedrooms were located.

Joe looked Halleigh up and down, admiring her curves for the first time. "Yeah, you gon' heat things up quite a bit with your rays, Sunshine." Joe smiled at Halleigh, caressing her chin with his index finger. "My boy gon' love you, ma." He licked his lips and turned to Mimi. "You, princess, come with me." Looking over at Halleigh, he said, "And you can wait in here for my boy. Just chill out and relax. My man should be here any minute. Get yourself a drink or something in the meantime. But take care of my young boy for me, all right?"

Halleigh nodded her head in agreement and then watched as Mimi and Joe left the room.

* * *

Tariq and Malek pulled up to Jamaica Joe's house and noticed the group of people headed inside. Everyone who was invited to the party was a close friend or associate of Joe's. They were people he trusted, so Malek wasn't worried about any drama popping off inside. He knew that he couldn't take his gun inside of Joe's house—house rule—so he took it out of his waistline and stored it under Tariq's passenger's seat.

Malek got out of the car and followed Tariq up the driveway, limping slightly, making him seem a bit more gangster than he actually was. Malek had been anything but gangster up until a year ago when circumstances changed his situation.

Before getting into the drug game, the only game Malek had ever concerned himself with was the game of basketball. And although new to the game, the bullet he had taken for Jamaica Joe was getting him much respect from the entire North Side of Flint.

Tariq and Malek walked up to the back door, where they were greeted by a member of their crew. They walked inside and greeted Jamaica Joe, who had just returned from the back bedroom. Mimi was on his arm.

Joe released Mimi and then slapped hands with Malek and embraced him tightly. "I got a surprise for you, baby," he stated. He slapped hands with Tariq and said, "Get on the door. You know who gets in and out."

Tariq sniffed loudly as he scratched his nose and nodded his head. He was tired of being treated like a flunky. It was like Malek had become Joe's favorite soldier. Tariq kept his feelings inside and stood by the back door as he was instructed, while he watched Malek join the party inside.

Joe threw his arm around Malek and led him through the house, toward the back bedroom. "How that leg feeling?"

"It's all right," Malek responded, tapping his leg. "It keeps me standing. And I guess that's all that matters, that I'm still standing. Some ain't so lucky." Malek put his head down.

It was obvious to Joe that he was referencing his mother and stepfather. "I heard that," Joe said. "And, yo, you know we gon' handle that shit with your moms and pops and shit. I'm sorry your family got pulled into all this."

Malek simply nodded, not wanting to think anymore about the great loss he'd suffered. He had already lost a part of his heart when Halleigh disappeared. The other part had been stripped from him the day his mother and stepfather were taken from this earth. And as far as Malek was concerned, his stepfather, in his heart, was his real father. After all, he was the man who had raised him ever since he married Malek's mother when Malek was only eight years old. Malek's biological father had gotten himself killed in a drug deal gone bad; not that his sorry ass had ever played a part in Malek's life before his death anyway.

"I got something to cheer you up, though," Joe stated with a mischievous smile. "It's right in this room." He pointed to one of the bedroom doors then patted Malek on the shoulder. "Don't hurt yourself, li'l man," he added as he walked away, knowing that the young girl was about to put it on Malek.

Malek opened the door and saw a girl sitting on the bed. She was bent over, her face buried in her hands. He could see her body trembling, and she seemed to be in deep thought.

Feeling a presence in the room, the girl looked up and straight into Malek's eyes. Malek couldn't believe the sight before him. He stood there in complete disbelief. *This isn't real.* Then finally he spoke. "Halleigh?" Malek called out in astonishment.

The sound of his voice let her know that her eyes hadn't deceived her. Tears flooded her line of sight as she ran to him. He hugged her tightly, picking her up off her feet.

Halleigh pulled back and touched his face, allowing her rich persimmon-complected fingers to run the course of his dark sienna-brown skin. She ran her hands down the ripples of waves in his hair. She just wanted to make sure that he was real. Once she was completely convinced, she pressed herself back up against him.

For all this time, Halleigh had felt so much anger toward Malek. She wanted to be mad at him forever. But as he stood in front of her in the flesh, that deep-seated love she had for him outweighed every other emotion.

As Malek held her, she felt relief swarm over her body. Just being in his arms again made everything okay. He was the answer to all of her prayers. For a minute, Halleigh forgot all about the past year. She forgot all about the life she was living, and that she was at that house on an assignment. She felt like the smart high school girl that she had once been; untainted by the streets.

"Baby," was all Malek said as he kissed her on top of her head, which was buried in his chest. Halleigh began to sob hysterically as he held onto her and tears came to his own eyes. Malek squeezed her even tighter against him, as if she might disappear any second.

"I thought you left me," she cried hysterically. "You left me."

"Shhh. I would never leave you, Hal. I thought you left me," he told her. "Do you know that? I looked for you every day for weeks." He rubbed her hair softly, trying to soothe her soul. He had no idea of the things she had experienced since he'd last seen her, but he could feel that there was something different about her.

He put her back down to her feet and looked her in the eyes. She was still the most beautiful girl he had ever seen, but she looked tired and worn down, the small bags underneath her eyes revealing nothing but sadness and despair.

"What happened to you? Where have you been?" he asked. "I thought I saw you one day, but..." Malek's words just trailed off. He was still in disbelief.

Halleigh stared at him blankly. She knew it was about to start: him asking her twenty-one questions. But Halleigh didn't know if she should lie or tell the truth. She couldn't help but wonder if she told him about the person she was now, would he still love her?

"You just up and dipped on me," Malek stated when Halleigh never responded.

"I dipped on you?" Halleigh couldn't believe he had just fixed his lips to say that. "You're the one who left me stuck here while you ran off out of town without me." That old anger began to rear its ugly head in Halleigh's tone. She poked Malek in the chest as she spoke her next words. "You promised me you would take me away from here. You promised you would be there for me. You lied and it's been hell. I've been out here all alone trying to survive. You have no idea what I've been through since you left me. No idea." Tears flooded Halleigh's eyes.

Malek tried to reach out to her, but she pulled from his reach. "You hurt me, Malek." She flopped down on the bed hopelessly as hot tears flowed uncontrollably. Her spirit felt so broken and confused that she couldn't think straight. She had imagined the moment that she would be reunited with Malek so many times, but now that he was in her presence, she didn't know what to say or do.

Malek let out an "are you kidding me?" chuckle.

"What are you talking about, Hal? I never left town." Malek kneeled down in front of her.

"Then why didn't you come for me? I came to your house and your mother told me everything."

A perplexed look covered Malek's face. "What do you mean, *everything*?"

"That you were gone. She said that you didn't want to see me. That you blamed me for losing your shot at going pro. Malek, you don't know half the things I've had to go through this past year." Halleigh stood up and walked away in shame. She didn't even want Malek to be able to look into her eyes and see who she was now. "You have no idea." Halleigh just shook her head and continued to cry.

Malek took a deep breath and swallowed the disappointment that was stirring up in him. The last thing he wanted to do was to feel anger toward his deceased mother, but he could only imagine the conversation that took place between her and Halleigh. He could only imagine the lies his mother had fed her just to keep the two of them apart. But he loved his mother dearly. He couldn't get upset with her, especially now that she was dead. All the good his mother had done for him in his life could never outweigh the bad. All his mother ever wanted was what was best for Malek, and she had worked hard to make sure that he got it.

When Malek was just a baby, his mother would put in long hours, working two and three jobs at a time if she had to, just so she wouldn't become a statistic. She did not want to be a young, single mother raising her child on welfare, which was the life her own mother had lived. She didn't want her child to experience the embarrassment and humiliation that she did as a child on welfare.

One day when Malek's mother was in first grade, she experienced what she thought was the most embarrassing moment in her life. She was in the grocery store line with her mother when one of her classmates got in line behind them with her mother.

When it was their turn to get checked out, Malek's mother wanted to disappear when her mother pulled out all of those books of food stamps to pay for the grocery bill. By the time Malek's mother arrived at school the next morning, the entire class knew that she was on food stamps. The jokes followed her all the way through elementary. It was a childhood scar she carried with her all through her life, right up to the birth of Malek.

She swore that she would do whatever it took to stay off of welfare. So, not once in her life did she ever receive government assistance. And on top of working so hard, she still managed to be there to support Malek in everything he did. Some days she didn't even get a moment's rest. It was something that wore her body out physically, but more than anything, it was something she was proud of. And not one time did she ever fuss, holler or complain about the sacrifices she had made. She knew that Malek making it into the NBA and making enough money to take care of her for the rest of her life was her reward. That's when she would rest. But now, she was resting in peace, and Malek would respect that rest by instantly forgiving his mother for keeping him away from Halleigh.

Malek put his hands on both sides of Halleigh's face and made her look him in the eyes. "Look, Hal, a lot of shit has happened in my life since the last time I saw you." He paused for a moment. "I met Jamaica Joe while I was in the county jail that day of the robbery. He hooked me up with a lawyer that took care of the case for me. It was thrown out. Me and Joe been tight ever since. I mean, if it hadn't been for him, I could still be rotting in jail somewhere. But because I'm associated with him, I've made some enemies." Malek paused for a moment and then continued. "I got popped last year during the Berston game in a shoot-out between Joe and this nigga named Sweets from the North Side."

Halleigh interrupted. "I was there that day. Oh my God. I was there," she exclaimed. She couldn't believe she had been in the same vicinity as Malek and didn't even know it. She had always felt as though they were soul mates, and that she would just be able to sense that he was around. But after all, her mind was cloudy that day. That would be the first time Halleigh worked as a Manolo Mami. She was set to turn her first trick that day. If only she had found Malek that day, so much in her life could have been different. She would never have turned that first trick; a trick that led to another and then another, getting her to the point where she was today . . . a bonafide whore.

"You were there at the park that day?" Malek said as a gleam shot across his face. "I knew it. I thought I saw you there. I though that was you. I knew it."

"Then why didn't you say anything?"

"Because when I saw you, that's when all that shit start jumpin' off, you know. One of Sweets' li'l niggas got hit." Malek paused again, fighting back tears. "Well, I got hit in my calf and the hip. But they didn't hit no major arteries or nothing, so I was good. But after hearing about my injuries, my basketball career wasn't good, if you know what

I'm saying. My agent dropped me; not a single school was interested in me any longer. It was a trip."

"I'm sorry to hear that, Malek," Halleigh said sincerely. "I know making it to the pros was everything for you."

"Yeah, well, at least I still have my life." Malek sighed. "I can't say the same for moms and pops."

"What–what happened?" Halleigh stammered.

"To top off everything that was going on, someone sprayed my house, and my moms and pops got hit. They, uh, they, uh, they dead."

Halleigh's mouth dropped in shock. She couldn't help but allow her mind to go back to the root of the chain reaction of bad stuff that had taken place in Malek's life. She shook her head, knowing that Malek's life had turned out badly because of her. That one night she went to Malek for help turned out to be what catapulted a life of destruction for both of them. All of this stemmed from her running to Malek for help that night after those two men raped her. *Why didn't I just run to the police?* Halleigh blamed herself.

"I'm sorry, Malek. I'm so sorry."

Halleigh walked back over to Malek, who was now sitting on the bed with his hands buried in his face. "I should have never even told you about me being raped that night. I should have just gone to the police and let them handle it. I mean, what was I thinking? You were just a high school kid. If you didn't try to help me, you wouldn't be where you are right now. You would be off somewhere playing hoop, and Mr. and Mrs. Johnson would still be alive. Maybe your mother was right—I was bad for you . . . I am bad for you."

Malek quickly uncovered his face. "That's the one thing that my moms was wrong about," he stated. "You're nothing but good for me." He finally got a smile from Halleigh, and a sexy smirk appeared on his lips as he pulled her wet face toward his and kissed her lips gently.

Halleigh escaped into good thoughts of her and Malek again as Malek made love to her with his mouth. His kiss felt like pure ecstasy to her. It had been a long time since a man kissed her the way Malek kissed her . . . and didn't have to pay for it.

Malek's kisses now felt different to Halleigh. He was more mature and had developed a thug demeanor. But Halleigh liked it. She loved it. She loved her some Malek, and that was just something that would never go away.

After their kiss ended, Halleigh turned her back to him. "Things are different now, Malek. You don't know how much has happened to me," she mumbled, knowing that Malek wouldn't want her if he knew the truth; if he knew how many men she had let conquer her body, something he had never done. Not once had she and Malek ever been intimate together, and she just knew he wouldn't be able to deal with hearing how many men had touched her in a way that he 'had never touched her.

"Then tell me." Malek turned Halleigh back around to face him. "Make me understand."

Halleigh opened her mouth, but nothing came out. She just shook her head. "I can't. You won't want me," she whispered painfully as shameful tears continued to flow freely.

"I'll always want you. I've always wanted you," he assured her. "You don't know how long I looked for you after I got out of jail and the hospital. I love you, Halleigh. I'll always want you in my life. Don't be afraid to share who you are with me. I mean, I'm not the same Malek you knew either. You may not agree with some of the stuff I've been into, but if we are going to make this thing work, we have to share with each other who we are. Now tell me. What's going on with you, Halleigh?" He looked deep into her eyes. "Tell me who you are."

Halleigh's body shook as she thought about all the different men, all the abuse, and all the manipulation she went through because of Manolo. She opened her mouth, and this time, she proceeded to tell Malek everything about the life she was now living.

"After Mrs. Johnson told me that you left town, I didn't have anywhere to go. The day before, I had met this girl named Mimi at the police station, where I had been waiting for you to get released. She told me that her daddy might be able to help me out with a place to stay and coming up with some money toward your bail. I went home with her and met him. I didn't know that when she called him *Daddy*, she was referring to her pimp."

"Pimp?" Malek exclaimed.

Halleigh didn't respond.

"Some nigga out here putting you up for sale?" he asked angrily.

"I didn't know, Malek. It was too late. I got trapped in the life. And after I thought you had abandoned me, I just felt so lost and alone that I didn't even care anymore. I didn't care about myself." Halleigh swallowed and continued. "He promised to take care of everything for me, and he put a roof over my head. But I swear to you, Malek, I didn't realize what I was getting myself into until it was too late. Now I can't get out. He'll kill me."

Her story brought tears of anger to Malek's eyes. For him, all of this was like dèj vu. Once again, someone had taken advantage of Halleigh's innocence, the innocence that had rightfully belonged to him. The innocence he waited for until she was ready. The thought of her being manipulated into selling her body to other men, any man, sickened and angered Malek. He balled his hands into fists and leaned over the bed as he rested, hitting himself in the head out of frustration.

Finally, through gritted teeth, he asked Halleigh, "How many niggas?"

Halleigh was stunned by Malek's question. She couldn't understand why he would want to know the intimate details. It would only hurt him the same way it hurt her just thinking about it. Although Halleigh felt that her mother held a big part of the blame for her being on the streets, she somehow felt like she was worse than her mother. She had watched her mother do a lot of things to get high. She lied, cheated and stole. She was such a good booster that she could steal the Pope's hat off of his head on national television without anyone noticing. But not once . . . not once had Sharina sold her own body to get high. *No, she just sold mine,* Halleigh reasoned, *and now I'm keeping it going.*

"Answer me. How many men, Halleigh?" Malek repeated, trying to maintain his composure.

Halleigh just stood there shaking her head.

"How many men?" Malek finally yelled.

Malek's booming tone startled Halleigh and she quickly said, "I don't know. I don't know how many, Malek. I lost count," Halleigh confessed. "When I'm doing it, I just blank out and try to imagine that I'm somewhere else." She closed her eyes. "Somewhere else . . . with someone else . . . like with you."

Malek was silent as he tried to process what she had just told him. "What's the nigga's name that got you out here like this?" he asked. He knew that he could call in a favor from Joe and get the situation handled, but this shit was personal. Malek was gonna take care of the dude that had Halleigh trickin' on the streets himself, he thought as his nose flared.

Halleigh could practically hear his thoughts. "No, Malek. Please . . . I don't want to pull you into anything else. I've already messed up your life."

"What's his name?" Malek asked her again, his tone hard. "What's his name, Halleigh?" he yelled.

"Manolo," she whispered.

The look on Malek's face said it all. "You a Manolo Mami?" he asked in disgust. He knew Manolo's reputation in the pimp game. He knew Manolo was all about the paper and kept his girls working. He couldn't help but think of all the niggas that Halleigh had given herself to. *How did I let this happen to her?*

"I'm sorry," she whispered. "I'm so sorry. Please don't hate me. I know you probably think I'm dirty now, but please, Malek, please . . ."

Malek wanted to embrace Halleigh, but he couldn't move. He was sick just thinking about how many niggas had been with her. He gagged inside as tears rolled down his face.

"Malek?" Halleigh said. "Please say something . . . anything."

Malek swallowed his tears and regained his composure. He wiped his face dry and then sniffed, standing there as if he had never been crying. He then looked over to Halleigh and softly summoned her. "Come here."

Halleigh almost didn't hear him, so he said it again.

"Come here, girl. You don't have nothing to be sorry about." They met each other halfway, and once again, he held her tightly in his arms. "I shouldn't have let this happen to you. But don't you worry. I said I'd always be here for you. That ain't changed. I'ma handle this," he responded, glaring off with a look of hatred and revenge in his eyes. "You best believe I'ma handle this."

"Malek, can we get out of here? I can't do this anymore. I can't do this."

"I got you, Halleigh. You leaving with me. I'ma take care of you this time." And he meant it. He pulled her close to him. If he had to use every dime he had saved up since working for Joe, he was going to take care of Halleigh. He wiped the tears from her face, and she rested her head against his chest. "I'ma take you far away from Flint. Ain't nobody gon' hurt you again."

Chapter Seven

"I'm about to murder this nigga." Lynch leaned up from the back seat, in between the front car seats, where Sweets and Manolo were seated. Lynch had been on a mission of revenge ever since his brother, Rah-Rah, was shot and killed at the Berston Park shootout. He took his initial anger out on the easiest target, Malek's house. As far as he was concerned, the North Side/South Side war had just begun. Joe had taken out one of their boys, so in return, one of his boys had to get taken out. It was his brother, his flesh and blood, that had been killed. He wanted Joe's head on a platter, and if he had to take out all of his crew just to get to the captain, so be it.

"Yeah, whatever. Just make sure you don't pop off before I get the combo to the safe," Sweets stated calmly to Lynch as they prepared to head to Joe's.

The Shottah Boyz, Sweets' young hit squad, sat in the back seat. Once a four-member clique, there were now only three young killers since the death of Rah-Rah, the craziest, stone-cold killer of them all.

Everyone's eyes were concentrated on the luxury house in front of them. The lights were on throughout the house, and they could hear the loud music coming from within. The loud music seemed awkward in the suburban neighborhood.

The only person standing outside was Tariq. Every so often, he stepped outside and walked around to scope things out. And when he came around the house and spotted Sweets in an SUV, he nodded, giving them the green light to bring it on.

They all felt the adrenaline pumping in their veins. The group of men made sure that the safeties were disabled on their weapons. They didn't want to take any chances. Whoever got in the way would get popped that night.

Lynch was especially ready. Since the death of his brother, he hadn't been the same. His murder game had become out of control as he tried to quench his thirst for death. He was taking out niggas left and right just for looking at him funny. He was like that dude Larenz Tate played in the movie *Menace II Society*. He felt as though he didn't have anything to lose. When he lost his brother, he lost everything, as far as he was concerned. And even though he had been leaving a path of death behind him, the only death that would truly mean something to him was Jamaica Joe's. He wanted Joe's head and knew that nothing would stop him from getting his revenge. Joe had been extremely careful, but Lynch knew that sooner or later he would get at him. The day had finally come.

"Yo, you sure this ain't a set-up?" Manolo asked Sweets as he stared suspiciously at the house, with Tariq casing back and forth.

"Shit, there's only one way to find out. Either way, I'm trying to get to what Joe got in that safe." Sweets pulled out a Blow Pop and stuck it in his mouth.

They slipped on their black ski masks and hopped out of the stolen SUV, leaving the ignition running for an easy getaway. They strolled up to the back door where Tariq was standing guard and eased right past him.

Tariq smirked and entered the house behind them, but instead of following them down the steps, he made his way upstairs and went into the bathroom. He waited patiently for shit to pop off.

Sweets bum-rushed the basement, his hit squad behind him.

As soon as Joe and his guests saw the masked intruders, screams erupted and the party came to a standstill.

"Put your mu'fuckin' hands up. Y'all already know what time it is," Sweets stated in a nonchalant tone as he pointed his 9mm at Joe and his guests. Manolo and the Shottah Boyz held all the guests at gunpoint.

Caught slipping, Joe gritted his teeth furiously. He immediately regretted throwing the party at his spot.

Sweets snatched Joe off the leather sectional and put the pistol to his head. "Where's the safe?"

Twenty minutes earlier, Mimi would have been sitting there clinging to Joe's arm, but she had to run out and get condoms. She had brought regular condoms with her, but Joe required Magnums, of which she had none. And if she'd learned anything from her years of trickin', it was never to let a nigga run up raw . . . no matter how much he was willing to pay.

"What you talking about, man? Ain't no safe in here." Joe was sweating bullets on the inside, but he wouldn't give anybody the pleasure of seeing him panic.

"Okay, so you wanna do this the hard way?" Sweets jammed his gun in Joe's neck and jerked him by the collar as he turned to face Lynch. "You see that nigga right there? He's waiting for me to give him the go-ahead. He is trying to get at you, for real. You took something away from him that he can't get back, nah mean?"

Joe stared at the man before him, but he couldn't see his face. It wasn't until he looked at his forearms that he saw the word *Shottah* tattooed in black ink. *Fuck,* he thought, knowing that the young boy before him was the brother of the nigga he'd murdered at Berston.

"Now, let's try this again. Where's the safe?"

Joe stood strong and still didn't respond.

Lynch, growing tired of Jamaica Joe's games, ran up on him and split his nose with the butt of his gun. "Nigga, you thinks this a game? Where the mu'fuckin' safe?" He whipped Joe across the face with the pistol two more times.

Jamaica Joe dropped to his knees in pain. He

held his face and blood seeped in between his fingers. He weighed his options and knew that he would have to reveal his safe to his intruders. *I got a pistol in that safe,* he thought. He knew that he was outnumbered greatly and began to regret not letting his boys enter his house with their pistols. One gun didn't amount to much, but he knew that it gave him a better chance of walking out of the situation with his life.

"It's underneath the floor," he stated as he got up and walked toward a bookshelf in the corner of the room.

"Hurry up." Sweets pushed Joe slightly, urging him to speed up the process.

Jamaica Joe pulled up some loose floorboards in his basement and revealed a steel combination safe. He paused, trying to buy more time. *How the fuck am I gon' get out of this? And where the fuck is Tariq?*

"Open it!" Sweets demanded.

Joe twisted the knob to the safe and opened the door, revealing the crystal-white cocaine inside.

"Load that shit up," Sweets ordered Joe then looked over to Lynch. "Handle your business, man," he stated, giving him the okay to shoot Joe.

Lynch raised his arm and aimed the .357 at Joe's head. Just as he was getting ready to pull the trigger, they heard a loud banging on the back door.

"Flint Police Department! Is anyone home?" the voice yelled loudly.

Sweets, Manolo, and the other two Shottah Boyz looked at each other nervously. They quickly snatched off their masks. "Block that mu'fucka," Sweets whispered, referring to the open safe, and Lynch quickly pushed the bookshelf over the missing floorboards.

Sweets put his finger to his lips, signaling for everyone in the basement to keep quiet.

Jamaica Joe never thought he would be so happy to have the cops at his door.

"Flint Police! We're coming in!" they shouted.

Jamaica Joe heard his back door open and shut. Sweets and his crew tried to hide their guns as the police came down the steps.

Two white cops came into the room. One immediately went to the home stereo system and cut the volume, and the other one looked around the room, his hand on his holster, looking for an excuse to open fire.

Even though Jamaica Joe's guests were afraid of Sweets and his crew, snitching was a no-no in Flint, so everyone kept their mouths shut and waited to see how the scene would play out.

"What seems to be the problem, officers?" Sweets asked, removing all traces of slang from his vocabulary.

"Are you the owner of this house?" one of the officers asked.

"No, sir," Sweets responded.

"Then who is?"

"I am," Jamaica Joe stated with a smile.

The officer frowned when he saw Joe's busted nose and asked, "Is everything all right here? What's going on?" He eyed the group of men suspiciously.

"I don't know." Jamaica Joe turned to Sweets. "Is everything all right?"

"Yeah, everything's cool, officer," Sweets responded. "Just a small gathering amongst friends, you know."

"Well, your gathering is disturbing your neighbors. We got a noise complaint, and it looks like we came just in time," one of the officers stated. The officers began their routine, separating Sweets and Jamaica Joe and questioning them to get to the bottom of the situation.

Jamaica Joe stared into the eyes of the white man as he used his shirt to wipe the blood from his nose.

"Now, if there is something going on here, you can tell me. If you need our assistance, all you have to do is nod your head," the officer stated.

"No, sir, our party just got a little out of control. I'm not feeling too well, though. I would appreciate it if you and your partner could clear this out for me." Joe stared intently across the room at Sweets and his crew. He was heated that they had the audacity to run up on him in his crib. The situation could have easily ended badly for him, so he was grateful for the lawful interruption.

"All right, it's time to clear this out. Party's over!" the officer yelled.

Joe's guests flew up the steps as quickly as possible. Nobody was trying to be a part of the bloodbath. Joe was so infuriated, he didn't realize that he was standing with his fists balled at his side.

The police officers stood and watched as Jamaica Joe walked over to Sweets and held up his hand, as if he were showing him love. Sweets looked at Joe's hand and then at the cops and decided that he would play along with Joe's little game. *Nigga, you got lucky this time, but next time I'ma make sure there are no interruptions.* He slapped Joe's hand.

Joe pulled Sweets toward him discreetly, but with force. "You niggas is dead."

Sweets and Joe stared each other down as they came out of their embrace. Sweets nodded his head to his crew, who were scared shitless. They all walked up the basement steps, while Joe remained in the basement, a cop on either side of him.

Rage overcame Joe as he witnessed Sweets and his crew walking out of his home with his bricks. He wasn't in a position to try to stop them, and his insides were boiling. He knew that he couldn't protest because of the cops' presence. Sweets gave Joe a small smirk like, *Yeah, I'm walking out with yo' shit and you can't do anything about it.* It took all of Joe's willpower not to grab Sweets up and take back what was his.

The cops were too busy directing people out of the house. They didn't notice the evil stares that Sweets and Joe were exchanging. If looks could kill, Joe and Sweets would both be circled in chalk.

As Sweets and his crew exited the door, Sweets looked back and held up the bags. "Yo, Joe, thanks for the party favors. That was very nice of you, buddy. Appreciate the hospitality," he said sarcastically as he made his way out of the door.

Just as Sweets, Manolo, and the Shottah Boyz reached the top of the steps, Malek and Halleigh walked out of the bedroom and through Joe's kitchen. With the loud music playing and their deep conversation, they hadn't heard the initial chaos and were clueless to the fact that robbery and murder had been about to go down.

Malek and Halleigh were prepared to exit through the back door when they bumped into Sweets, Manolo, and the Shottah Boyz. Halleigh stopped dead in her tracks when she saw Manolo's face. She tried to turn around, but it was too late.

"What the fuck are you doing here?" Manolo asked Halleigh, trying to disguise his anger because he knew the police were within earshot. He attempted to snatch Halleigh up.

But Malek slapped his hand with force. "Whoa, homeboy, you might want to calm that down if you know what's good for you. You don't got no business here no more." He pulled Halleigh close to him to show Manolo that he was serious. Malek could feel Halleigh's hand become moist as he held it in his.

"This one of our bitches?" Sweets asked Manolo as he eyed Halleigh, looking her up and down, making her feel as if she were naked. The disapproving tone in Sweets' voice let Manolo know he wasn't handling his business, embarrassing him.

Halleigh's breaths became shallow as she looked for an explanation. Finally she said, "Nolo, this is Malek. This is the guy that I needed the money for," she tried to explain.

Manolo leaned in close to her. "You remember what I told you when I first met you? You already know how I get down. You might get out of here tonight, but I'ma get at you, and when I do, I'm gon' kill the nigga right in front of you. I'm the Grim Reaper, baby girl. If you want this little nigga breathing, you better let him know who *Daddy* is."

Backed up on the stairs because of the scene that was occurring at the doorway, the police finally emerged from the basement. "Let's move it! Time to go!"

"Please, Manolo, don't do this," Halleigh begged.

Malek held onto her hand tightly as he waited for her to make a decision.

"You already know what it is," Manolo stated coldly as he walked out the door with Sweets, the Shottah Boyz, and the police following. "The ball is in your court now, Sunshine," he said, looking back at her over his shoulder.

Tears accumulated in Halleigh's eyes as she let go of Malek's hand. She knew that Manolo would kill him if she stayed. "I have to go," she whispered. "I'm sorry," she cried as she walked out the door.

"Halleigh!" Malek yelled as he stepped outside and watched her walk down the driveway, her head down. "Halleigh!"

The sound of his voice calling her name broke her heart. She looked back one last time. For a brief moment she contemplated running back into Malek's arms. He said he would take care of her, protect her, but he'd also said it the last time and didn't make good on his word. Could she trust him to protect her this time?

"Bitch, get in the car." Manolo got into the front seat of the SUV.

Halleigh's tears poured out of her eyes like flood

waters as she hopelessly got into the SUV. She watched Malek stand there in disbelief as Sweets drove away.

"Halleigh!" Malek started running toward the SUV in one last-ditch effort to get his girl.

Joe stopped him before he could get past him and just said, "Not now, kid. But don't worry. We gon' take care of this."

Halleigh had her face buried in her hands as she wept. She'd just done the hardest thing she ever had to do in her life. Turning her first trick wasn't even this hard. She loved Malek with all of her heart, from the depths of her soul, but out of fear for his well-being, she left with Manolo. She knew Manolo would follow up on his threat about killing Malek and didn't want that. What she didn't know was that Malek was no longer green to the streets and could hold his own. Nonetheless, she left the love of her life standing in heartbroken disbelief.

Chapter Eight

Jamaica Joe came out of the house to make sure that Sweets didn't try to double back. He walked to the end of his driveway and looked up and down the street, making sure that no odd cars were parked on the block.

Tariq and Mimi came running out of the house. Mimi had heard Manolo's voice when she came back in from the store after getting the condoms, so she ran for cover into one of the bedrooms. She'd thought about turning around and running back out of the house, but something inside of her just wouldn't let her leave Halleigh there. Actually, when she ran into the bedroom, she thought it was the one Joe had showed them to earlier, but it wasn't. Mimi stayed put and hid anyway until she thought the coast was clear.

"And where the fuck you been, mu'fucka?" Joe snapped. "How the fuck they ass get in my house?

You was supposed to be guarding the door!" Jamaica Joe yelled furiously as he pointed at Tariq's head.

Tariq's face showed surprise when he saw that Jamaica Joe was still alive. "I had to go take a shit, nigga. Damn! I had the bubble guts. How was I supposed to know that somebody was gon' run up in the spot?" Tariq asked. "Niggas ain't ever been that bold before." If Tariq hadn't really had the bubble guts before, he had them now. He couldn't believe the plan didn't go down smoothly, and now he was left standing with the possibility of Joe finding out that he was behind it all.

"How did they know where I lived?" Joe pretty much asked himself.

"You ain't been too cautious with that, fam," Tariq jumped in. "I mean, look how many niggas was up in your spot tonight. You used to be on it all the time, making sure just any and everybody didn't know where you rest at. But look, you throwing parties and shit. He could have found out easily," Tariq stated quickly, making sure that no suspicion was directed his way. He even went so far as to point a finger at Malek, who was sitting on the back steps, his head on his fists. "This nigga in love with one of the enemy's hoes, wifeying the bitch. She could've set the shit up."

"Shut the fuck up, nigga!" Malek jumped to his feet. "Don't speak my name, for real. That's just a warning for your best interests. Don't even speak her name."

"Oh shit!" Mimi said. "Where the fuck is Halleigh? Did she leave with them?" Mimi wrapped her arms around herself. She already knew the answer to her question, and she felt guilty because she knew that Halleigh was in for the beating of her life. And her too, if Halleigh told Manolo that it was Mimi who set up the entire thing.

"Yeah, ma, your girl left with them. It's time for you to bounce too." Joe pulled out three Gs and placed them in Mimi's hand.

Mimi stared at the money and then looked up at Joe. "Listen, I didn't have nothing to do with them coming here tonight."

"I know," Joe stated as he walked into his house.

"And how do you know that shit?" Tariq was quick to mention in an attempt to direct Joe's suspicions elsewhere.

" 'Cause my gut instincts tell me so," Joe said to Tariq. "The same instincts that done kept me around this long." Joe looked over at Mimi. "Go on, ma."

Right away, Mimi left, headed back to Manolo's house.

"Yo, Joe, man, I got to go get her." Malek was pacing, as if he wanted to follow Mimi to Manolo's and get Halleigh. "She needs my help. I can't just leave her."

"Man, fuck that bitch! You ain't Daddy no more, nigga," Tariq said. "Manolo pimpin' her ass all over town. She chose that life. We got bigger things to worry about for right now."

Joe hated to agree, but they had bigger fish to fry with Sweets' crew. "Yeah, I got to get back at them niggas. If I don't, South Side mu'fuckas gon' be trying to test me all the time. I got to make an example."

Malek thought about what Tariq and Joe had just said, and the longer he contemplated the situation, the angrier he became. He thought about all the things he had given up to be with Halleigh: forfeiting his future, trying to be her man and stand by her. His NBA career was non-existent because of his commitment to her. He'd even chosen to love her when his own mother hated her. He had sacrificed all those things, and she had the audacity to choose another nigga over him.

Maybe my moms was right. I can't fuck with Halleigh. I'm through. He joined Joe and Tariq in the house so that they could plan their next move.

Chapter Nine

"Manolo! She has to eat!" Tasha yelled as she walked behind him and pleaded on Halleigh's behalf. "You can't starve her, Manolo." She wanted desperately for him to ease up on his punishment of Halleigh, but every time Tasha came to Halleigh's defense, he would become even angrier.

"Shut the fuck up, Tasha, before you end up down there with her. I got to teach that bitch some discipline," he shot back. "Do you not understand what the fuck just went down tonight? For a little bit of paper, this bitch turned on us. She fucking with your reputation now, Tasha," Manolo said, trying to turn the tables on Tasha for not having the girls in check.

On that note, Tasha decided to fall back. She knew that she could be more of a help to Halleigh if she remained in Manolo's good graces.

Manolo was a cruel man and was showing exactly how devious he could be. After the botched robbery attempt at Joe's house he didn't say anything to her. Not one word. His silence was more threatening than his actual actions, though, because Halleigh knew that at any moment, when she was least expecting it, he could snap. And that's just what he did.

The morning after the party, while Halleigh was sitting down, preparing to eat the breakfast Tasha had prepared for the girls, Manolo snatched her up from the dining room table by her hair and dragged her to the basement, where he tossed her down the steps as if she were a rag doll. That was three days ago, and he hadn't let her out since.

Halleigh's stomach growled violently as a sign that she needed nourishment. She'd been in the damp, dark basement for days, and the only thing that she had to drink was the filthy water from the laundry basin. Halleigh had never experienced hunger pangs like the ones that raged throughout her body. She was famished and cried all day and all night for her punishment to end. Manolo forbade her to come up those steps and turn on the light switch at the top, so the only time she could see anything was during the day, when sunlight came through the sub-level windows.

At night, the basement was darker than dark, and she couldn't even see her own hand when she held it out in front of her. She constantly scratched her arms and legs as the dark played games on her. She always felt as if something was crawling on her. *All these spiders,* Halleigh thought as she scratched her body, breaking her skin and causing her arms to bleed. It was like being trapped in a dungeon.

"Manolo, please let me out," she pleaded from the bottom of the steps, just hoping and praying that the door would open, freeing her from the pits of hell. "Please, open the door!" she screamed.

Her cries were futile, because Manolo didn't budge. He kept her down there, locked up for her disloyalty. Halleigh was going crazy in her confinement. She began to talk to herself, pretending that she was having conversations with Malek.

As the days passed, she became weaker, and all she did was sleep. It was during that time that she began to dream of Malek. Thoughts of him were the only thing keeping her sane; thoughts of him coming to rescue her, and he didn't even know it.

Halleigh was aware that Malek would never be able to forgive her for what she had done. Her dreams would be the only place where they would ever be together, and she had to accept that. Her heart was shattered, and her spirit was broken. A part of her wished that she would just die down there. Manolo had made her feel worthless; the same tactic he'd used to trick her into becoming one of his girls in the first place.

Mimi could hear Halleigh crying at night when she slept in her bed, and the guilt was eating her alive. Halleigh hadn't even thought about ratting Mimi out to Manolo, so she took the punishment all herself. Her agonizing cries made Mimi's skin crawl, and she couldn't even imagine what Halleigh was going through.

After a while, Tasha began sneaking food and

water down to Halleigh when she felt the coast was
clear, which was only a couple of times. The smell
down there almost made Tasha sick to her stomach from Halleigh having to relieve herself in the
corner of the basement like she was a dog. But
Tasha was never bold enough to free Halleigh from
the basement.

Tasha would simply place food and water at the
bottom of the steps. She knew that Manolo had
gone crazy on Halleigh for making him look bad
in front of Sweets, and if he found out that Tasha
was feeding Halleigh, he might lock her up too.
But Tasha couldn't let Halleigh die from starva-
tion, so she took the risk anyway.

After almost two weeks of torture, Manolo finally
opened the door to the basement. "Halleigh?" he
called as he made his way down the steps.

Tasha and Mimi stood in the kitchen as they
waited anxiously for Halleigh to emerge.

"Halleigh?"

"Hmm?" she moaned.

Manolo saw her in a corner of the basement,
balled into a fetal position with her eyes closed.

"Halleigh!" he yelled, trying to get her attention. He walked over to her and picked her up.

She was too weak to object, even though she
didn't want his hands on her.

Her body flopped almost lifelessly as he carried
her up the steps. She stunk badly. Her monthly
cycle had come and gone, but the traces of blood
were dried up on her thighs and legs. The sun
burned her eyes when he stepped into the kitchen

with her. It was like a thousand needles were being stuck into them.

Mimi's hard exterior melted away when she saw her friend. She began to sob uncontrollably as Manolo carried Halleigh past her and into their room, where he just threw her down on the bed and left her.

Once Mimi saw Manolo exit the room, she immediately went back there. When she saw Halleigh, all she could do was just stand there and cry. She wanted to run over and hug Halleigh, but she looked so fragile that she might break if Mimi so much as touched her.

Tasha came into the room and comforted Mimi. She looked over at Halleigh in disbelief. *How could he do this to her?*

Manolo's deep voice startled both Tasha and Mimi as it boomed from the other room. "Clean her up for work tonight," he said then he left the house.

Mimi released herself from Tasha and then finally made her way over to Halleigh and kneeled by the head of the bed. "I'm so sorry, Hal. I'm so sorry."

Halleigh didn't respond. She couldn't speak as Mimi just kept apologizing over and over.

Mimi took a deep breath and then reached down into her bra. She pulled out the exact same hundred dollar bills that Joe had handed her the night of the party. "I got something for you," Mimi told Halleigh. "It's your pay from the party."

Halleigh just looked at Mimi, too weak to say anything.

"It's three thousand dollars," Mimi said truthfully. "I'll put it under your pillow. Okay?" As much as Mimi loved money, her conscience would not allow her to spend one dime of that money Jamaica Joe had paid her that night. And after all that Halleigh had endured at the hands of Manolo just because she was trying to help her out, Mimi felt that she owed it to Halleigh. That could have easily been her down there in that basement with Halleigh. If Mimi had learned anything in the game, it was that loyalty had a price. And this time, the loyalty that Halleigh had showed her would cost Mimi three thousand dollars, which she gladly paid.

Just then, Tasha came over and instructed Mimi to help her lift Halleigh. They carried her into the bathroom. Tasha ran bathwater while Mimi held Halleigh up. The two eventually got her clothes off and placed her into the water-filled tub. Tasha began to bathe Halleigh as if she were a baby. Halleigh just sat there with her eyes closed while Tasha rinsed the soap off of her. Tasha had to close her own eyes to stop the tears from falling.

When Halleigh finally did open her eyes, silent tears fell. She stared directly in front of her as Tasha tried to wash away her pain.

"Forget about that boy, Halleigh," Tasha told her. "Manolo will never let you leave now that he knows who you want to be with. I mean, that kid runs with Jamaica Joe for Christ's sake. Now you know he is off limits."

Halleigh was non-responsive.

"Manolo will never let you go," Tasha added. "He is jealous and crazy like that. He'll kill you before he gives you up to that boy. I'm not trying to see you in a box, Halleigh. Get it together before you leave him with no choice, sweetheart. You have to learn how to cope, baby, and learn fast, before you get seriously hurt." Tasha kissed the top of Halleigh's head and prayed to God that the young girl was listening.

Chapter Ten

"*You have to learn how to cope, baby, and learn fast, before you get seriously hurt.*"

Tasha's words echoed through Halleigh's head as she remembered their previous conversation. Halleigh had definitely found a way to cope, but now she was stepping her game up a notch, hoping for an even greater escape than her casual cocaine use had been providing her.

Halleigh tied the leather belt around her arm and found a large vein. She shook eagerly as she inserted the heroin needle into her arm. As she pumped the syringe into her system, her head fell back in satisfaction. All the ills of the world escaped her thoughts as she let the drug work its magic. Her heartbeat began to speed up, and all her worries went out of her body as she indulged in the most addictive drug ever created.

"Damn, Li'l Rina. You betta take it easy," Scratch said as he impatiently waited for his turn.

"Shut up, Scratch!" Halleigh shot back. "You said that it would make all the pain go away. Well, that's all I want to do." She passed the dirty needle back to Scratch.

Scratch didn't want to take it, but the urge was too strong. He felt guilty for turning Halleigh on to the poison, but she had come to him desperately seeking an escape from the world she was living in. And next to death itself, Scratch didn't know a better escape than heroin.

"This ain't for you, Li'l Rina. This ain't for you," he said as he filled the needle to the top and joined in on the party. Scratch looked at the beautiful young girl, and his conscience began to eat at him.

When Halleigh came to him crying about her life and how she had ended up living the life she was now living, just like Scratch had promised, he provided a listening ear. After Halleigh told him of her latest fiasco with Manolo, Scratch convinced Halleigh that drugs would help her through the pain. But he did it for his own selfish reasons. He needed a hit badly, and his listening ears only heard one thing while Halleigh spoke: an opportunity for himself. He knew that if he talked Halleigh into trying the drug, he could manage to get a free high out of the deal as well. But looking at Halleigh right now, none if it seemed worth it to Scratch anymore.

When Scratch looked at Halleigh, it was like déjà vu. He remembered how, years ago, it was her mother he had turned out on the drug. Unfortunately for Halleigh, history was repeating itself in a cruel way.

"You know you're too good for this life. You let Manolo go all upside yo' head, knowing that fool ain't no good. You don't need to be here with an ol' man like me. I already fucked up my life; I can't let you fuck up yours." Scratch tossed the needle down the alley. He was overcome with guilt and knew he wasn't right for feeding her poison.

"Scratch! What the fuck is wrong with you?" Halleigh yelled. Her eyes scanned the alley for the needle, and she quickly jumped up to fetch it. "I paid for that shit, and you throw it." Halleigh tried to scramble away, but Scratch grabbed her arm and pulled her back down. His eyes were watering, and Halleigh had never seen anyone look so sincere.

"Look, baby girl, this ain't for you. Look at yourself," Scratch told her. "I know I told you this shit would make you feel better, but I lied. Look at you. You're only worse."

"But I do feel better," Halleigh tried to convince Scratch. "It makes me better."

Scratch just looked at the monster he had created in Halleigh and shook his head. "I feel so bad for introducing this to you." Scratch dropped his head in shame. "Don't make the same mistakes that your momma made. She let life get the best of her, and now look at her. Get away from all this. Get away from me. Ol' Scratch ain't gon' do you no good. Scratch do more harm than good to anybody that comes into his life, it seems."

Scratch's words hit home for Halleigh, and it felt like her high left as the words came out of his mouth. The mention of her mother made Halleigh listen to what Scratch was saying. Was she like her mother? Was she letting this thing get to her and take over?

Halleigh was reminded of all the times she had witnessed her mother high. All the times her mother went out boosting clothes to keep up her habit. All the times her mother never came home after consecutive days of getting high. All the times her mother hadn't been there for her. And most importantly, the time her mother chose drugs over protecting her own daughter.

Scratch's words were, indeed, hitting Halleigh hard in the heart. She usually hated when he called her Li'l Rina because as far as she was concerned, she was nothing like her mother. But today she felt closer to her mother than she had in a long time. For the first time ever, she understood why her mother couldn't beat her addiction.

It took all Halleigh's might not to run and get the needle that Scratch had tossed, but she took a step back and looked at herself. *What the fuck am I doing? Am I an addict now? I can't help it, though. It feels so good. I just don't want to feel bad anymore. I just want to feel good.*

"I have to go, Scratch. Time to get back to work," Halleigh said as she left Scratch alone in the alley. She hated her new habit, but it helped her get through the day. When she was high, it made the tricks she turned seem like a blur. She liked it better that way. The demons that haunted her 19-year-old soul were enough to drive a sane person crazy. Halleigh had fallen at the hands of the game.

Scratch, feeling lower than ever, watched as Halleigh walked off. It hurt him to his heart that he'd turned another woman onto his preferred drug. He was responsible for starting Halleigh's mother on drugs. Although he hadn't seen Sharina in ages, it still bothered him to this day that he had ruined her life. Scratch watched Halleigh until she faded away, and then ran over to retrieve the heroin needle he had thrown.

"I'm sorry, Halleigh," he whispered.

Chapter Eleven

As Halleigh headed back to the hotel, she tried to conjure up an excuse for being gone so long. She couldn't tell Tasha that she was out doing drugs with Scratch in an alley, so her mind raced, trying to figure out a legit story. Manolo kept close tabs on his girls, and if the money didn't add up at the end of the night, there would definitely be a price to pay. As far as Halleigh was concerned, she had paid her share to the piper, and there was no way she was going to set herself up to endure any more torment at the hands of Manolo.

What the fuck can I tell her? I've been gone for hours and shot all of my money up in my veins? I don't know . . .

Before Halleigh could finish her thought, she got an idea. She turned around and headed back to the alley. When she got there, she found Scratch pushing the last of the drug from the needle into his veins. "Want to make some money?" she asked Scratch.

"Do pigs oink?" was his reply. "Hell yeah, Scratch wanna make some money!"

"I got an idea. Follow me," Halleigh said as she led him back to her hotel.

Halleigh rested her hand on the telephone, making sure that Scratch understood what to say. "Make sure you repeat it just like I told you," Halleigh instructed.

"Scratch got it, baby girl."

"Tell her that you've got a thousand dollars for a bitch with a mean head job and to meet you in the lobby," she said, coaching Scratch.

"Cool."

Halleigh picked up the phone and dialed Mimi's room number and quickly handed the phone to Scratch.

Scratch cleared his throat and waited to hear a voice on the other end. After the fifth ring, Scratch heard a woman's voice answer the phone. "Looky here, baby girl," Scratch started. "I'm looking for a bitch with a mean head game. Dig this: I got a thousand dollars for whoever can show me a good time."

Halleigh stood there watching intensely as Scratch tried to sound as smooth as he could in his short conversation with Mimi. Halleigh could tell that back in the day, Scratch definitely had game. And she could tell by the look on his face that he enjoyed pretending to go back in time and play the role.

After he finished his conversation, Scratch hung up the phone and licked his lips, feeling good about what he had just done. He thought he still had game, and in his mind, his slick talking confirmed it.

"What did she say?" Halleigh asked impatiently as she threw her hands up.

"You know ol' Scratch is nice with the ladies. She was hanging off my every—"

"What the fuck did she say? Damn!" Halleigh snapped, cutting Scratch off, hoping that he would just get to the point.

"She said she'll meet me in the lobby in five minutes," Scratch said smoothly. He continued to smile and rub his hands together like a 1980s pimp.

"Good." Halleigh ran to her peephole and waited to see Mimi walk past, on her way down to the lobby. She knew that Mimi secretly took calls to do side jobs without Tasha knowing. She figured that Mimi was too greedy to let the opportunity pass to make that much money.

Right on cue, Mimi rushed down to the lobby. Halleigh knew she didn't have a lot of time before Mimi would get tired of waiting for the john that would never come, and she would eventually return back to her room.

Halleigh rushed to the door that joined their two rooms and entered Mimi's room. She searched Mimi's drawers, underneath the bed, and her purse, looking for Mimi's money.

"Damn!" Halleigh yelled after a few minutes of searching and not coming up with anything. Her eyes nervously scanned the room, trying to figure out just where Mimi's stash could be. She knew Mimi hadn't taken it with her. The girls knew better than to carry their money on them. More than a few johns had tried to rob their tricks before, and Mimi was in the game long enough to know better.

Halleigh picked up the mattress and flipped it over and still found nothing. *Damn! I know she didn't take her money with her, this time of all times,* she thought as the realization sunk in. Her plan had failed. She would have no money to turn over to show that she'd been working all day. She would have to suffer the consequences with Manolo. Hopefully it wouldn't be more time in the basement.

Just as Halleigh turned to exit the hotel room, she saw a bulky Newport cigarette box on the dresser and thought, *Bingo!* Halleigh rushed over to the box and opened it up, feeling like she'd hit a Vegas jackpot. There was Mimi's money, rolled up and stuffed into that cigarette box.

"Ooh, Mimi, girl, I told you smoking was bad for your health." Halleigh shrugged as she scooped the box up from the dresser and rushed out of Mimi's hotel room and back over to her own, through the same connecting door she had entered.

There, Scratch was waiting, hoping that Halleigh's scheme had worked, so that at least this time he wouldn't have to worry about where the money for his next hit was coming from.

Halleigh closed the door and walked over to Scratch. "Here!" she said as she pulled the money out of the box and handed him two balled-up twenties.

Scratch's face lit up. He hadn't had that much money all at one time in weeks. "Good lookin' out, Li'l Rina," Scratch said, holding one of the twenties up in the air, examining it and then plucking it.

Halleigh rushed Scratch out of the room so that she could make her way over to Tasha's room to show her just how much money she had made since she'd been gone. She told him, "Look, I'll see you later."

When Halleigh got to Tasha's door, she flattened down her clothes and relaxed her shoulders. She then held her hand up to the door. Just before she knocked, a streak of guilt went through her like lightning. *How can I do this to Mimi?* she asked herself. Halleigh knew what was going to happen to Mimi if she didn't have any money to show for her time today. Knowing darn well that Tasha had tabbed all of her tricks, Manolo wasn't going to accept any excuses as to why she didn't have his money. But then Halleigh thought about another day in that basement. Next she thought about how Mimi, knowing she was the one to blame, didn't have any problem letting her ass stay down there to be tortured. *I didn't see her ass stepping up to my rescue.* Halleigh knocked on Tasha's door.

Tasha yelled, "Come in."

As Halleigh walked in, another one of Manolo's girls was heading out. There were about five other girls in the room, including Tasha. Halleigh brushed past the girl who was leaving and walked over to Tasha. She was sitting at the table counting money.

"You in trouble," Tasha said in a low voice, never even taking her eyes off the money she was counting. "I told you about disappearing." She pushed her bangs off her forehead and allowed them to blend in with her layered hair.

Before Halleigh could respond, Manolo came out of the bathroom, making Halleigh's heart skip a beat. She didn't expect him to come all the way across town to check up on the girls. He seldom came to the regular hotel where the girls turned all their tricks.

"Where the fuck have you been all day?" Manolo spat. "Tasha said you didn't check in or nothing." He walked over to Halleigh, chest puffed up in an intimidating manner.

Halleigh pulled Mimi's earnings out of her pocket and said, "I've been working. I went to the store to get something to eat and I got approached by a couple of johns. I made the money right then and there because they weren't trying to come back to the hotel."

"That's my bitch," Manolo said proudly. *Maybe she's finally coming around,* he thought.

He looked down at his watch. "It's time for me to wrap it up for the night. I'll meet y'all at home. Tasha, collect the money and have it counted before y'all get home, baby." He pulled Tasha up and kissed her passionately on the lips, smacking her ass when he finished.

He walked over to Halleigh and did the same to

her. He thought about the wad of money she'd just turned over. "You made Daddy proud today, Sunshine."

When Manolo left the room, Tasha returned her full attention to Halleigh. She noticed that something was different about her. Her eyes were moving fast, and she couldn't stay still. "Are you okay, Hal?" Tasha asked in a soft, concerned tone. "You don't look so good."

"Yeah. Why you ask that? I'm good." Halleigh said, trying to look as normal as she possibly could. *Damn! Can she tell that I'm high? I don't look high, do I?*

Boom!

The door banged against the wall as Mimi stormed in the room totally enraged. "Somebody stole my mu'fuckin' money!" she yelled as she balled up her fist. "I know it was one of y'all bitches!" she said loud enough for all the girls to hear, even the one who went into the bathroom when Manolo had come out.

"Calm down yo' voice! Don't bring that shit up in here," Tasha said low, but stern.

"Tash, my fault," Mimi said. "But my money is gone. I just made a run to the store, and when I came back, it was gone."

"I don't have anything to do with that. You have to explain that shit to Manolo." Tasha continued to count the money.

"I swear to God, it's some fake-ass bitches in here! When I find out who got my shit, I'm beating a bitch's ass!" Mimi stormed out of the room, knowing she had to try to make some money before she saw Manolo. She didn't want him to beat her ass, so she knew she had to get her hustle on.

Halleigh took a deep breath. She hated that she'd smoked up all her money and had to steal Mimi's, putting her in jeopardy. But just as quickly as the last wave of guilt had disappeared, so did this one.

Whatever. Just like when she left me on stuck at Jamaica Joe's house, I'ma let her ass take the fall for this one. I got to do whatever I got to do to get by. Halleigh took another deep breath and returned to her room.

Chapter Twelve

Mimi and Tasha started to notice a drastic change in Halleigh's behavior and appearance. She was always so edgy and "noided" and was losing weight by the hour, it seemed.

The three of them had grown close living under the same roof together, but lately, Halleigh was acting all paranoid. She was acting withdrawn, and seemed spaced-out all the time. She was often depressed, and when she thought no one was paying attention, she cried silently to herself.

"I mean, let's just leave her alone. Let her do her. Maybe she ain't trying to have us all up in her face," Mimi stated one day when Tasha asked her opinion on the situation. She figured that Halleigh would eventually snap out of whatever it was she was going through.

Tasha knew that there was much more to the story. Her heart went out to Halleigh because she could see what the streets were doing to her. Ho'ing was sucking the life right out of Halleigh. Tasha could see Halleigh's innocence fading, and the youthful sparkle in her eye had disappeared completely.

Since Halleigh's run-in with Malek, she had lost all hope. Not once had he come for her. It wasn't that she really wanted him to come knocking down the door and making a scene, because the last thing she wanted was for him to once again put his life on the line for her. But if Julia Roberts could dream about her Prince Charming in the movie *Pretty Woman*, couldn't Halleigh?

After all, Malek was real to her. He was once her Prince Charming. He was all that she had ever wanted, but the reality was, they would never be together. After all that had happened, it was impossible for them to reconnect. Things would never go back to the way they used to be. Manolo had made it clear that she was not to associate herself with Malek, and if she disobeyed, he would kill both her and Malek.

Halleigh's appreciation for Manolo had long ago turned into contempt. She hated the sight of him, and the sound of his voice made her sick to her stomach. In her eyes, he was the root of all evil. He held her life in his hands and was unwilling to let her go. Halleigh knew that getting away from him would be one hell of a fight—a fight she just didn't have the energy for.

"I should just kill Manolo's ass." Halleigh thought out loud in desperation as she lay in the bed in one of her depressed states.

Mimi exited the bathroom just in time to hear Halleigh's outburst. She snapped her head in Halleigh's direction, a look of shock on her face. Then she rushed to their bedroom door and closed it. *I hope Manolo didn't hear that,* she thought.

Mimi walked back over to Halleigh and sat next to her. "Girl, you better stop talking reckless before somebody hears you," she whispered. "Have you lost your mind?"

Halleigh didn't say a word to Mimi. She just sat Indian-style and closed her eyes, like it was too painful for her to see her life as it was.

"What is wrong with you?" Mimi asked.

"I just want to be with him. Malek is all that I know. He is my heart. We had plans that always included each other. He's all I've ever really wanted." She dropped her head and played with her fingernails. "He's how I ended up here in the first place. I was just trying to help him, earn a little money to help put up toward his bail, but look at me now, Mimi. Look at me now. I'm a whore! Who wants to spend the rest of their life with a whore who almost every nigga in Flint done ran up in, huh?"

Mimi looked at Halleigh with sympathy, but she couldn't feel empathy. She knew that Halleigh was in love with Malek. She could always tell when Halleigh was thinking about that boy, and that was usually day in and day out, but Mimi couldn't fathom having love for another person. The only person she cared about was herself, not because she was selfish, but because she knew no other way.

Mimi's mother had abandoned her when she was just a child, sending her into the foster care system at the tender age of three. Never having a stable environment took its toll on Mimi. She never stayed in the same place long enough to develop any attachments, and she practically raised herself.

"Shit, I can't really speak on that because I don't know nothing about love. The only thing I love is money. If a nigga got money, I guess I could learn to love him too."

Halleigh shook her head. "No, you don't know anything about the way I feel because money can't compare to Malek. I would die for him."

"You are basically dying for him. The only reason you still here is to stop Manolo from hurting that boy. You saving his life and he don't even know it."

Yeah, if only he knew, Halleigh thought. *If only he knew.*

Chapter Thirteen

Sweets sat back and watched one of his many boyfriends as he counted his money. He had quickly unloaded all of the bricks that he had stolen from Jamaica Joe, and the profit was incredible. He hated to admit it, but Joe had a nice connect and the quality of his heroin was better. *No wonder I can't keep up with this nigga,* Sweets thought as he concentrated on the different denominations that he flipped through his hands. The process was lengthy because most of the bills were wrinkled fives, tens, and twenties. It was money that had probably been everywhere, from stuck down in a sock to the crotch of a G-string. But he couldn't complain. He knew that dirty money was the best money, and he loved getting it.

But what he could complain about was Joe. He was tired of sharing the city with Joe and knew that it was only a matter of time before he crushed Joe's North Side empire.

What gave Sweets the advantage in the battle was that Jamaica Joe wasn't even aware that there was a snake in his camp. *He should've made sure he was feeding his soldiers. If niggas ain't eating, they start creeping. Disloyal-ass nigga,* Sweets thought. He hated workers like Tariq. He felt that a side needed to be chosen. Either you were North or South. He despised dudes that tried to ride the fence. Usually, Sweets would have murked any nigga who tried to step to him with any type of proposition such as the one Tariq had presented him with. But Tariq was different. He was Joe's right-hand man, not just some disgruntled corner boy, and he knew the ins and outs of Joe's operation. So Sweets used it to his advantage. He was going to get as much information from Tariq as he could and then dispose of him afterwards.

Sweets sucked on the Blow Pop in his mouth as he reached for his twin Desert Eagle pistols and looked around his bedroom. He placed one pistol in his lap and put the other on the nightstand next to him.

"Ay, go check the door," Sweets instructed his lover.

"I just did an hour ago," was the gentleman's reply.

"Then get your ass up and do it again and shut them dick suckers up."

Sweets had been on edge ever since hitting Joe's spot. He knew that Joe wasn't going to let the situation go easily. He would try to retaliate, but when he did, Sweets planned on being prepared. *He won't catch me slipping,* Sweets thought.

Most dudes who were out in the open with their attraction to other men would have been underestimated when it came to gunplay, but Sweets was amongst the feared in Flint. It wasn't a secret that he had been with both men and women, but preferred men to women any day. He had been gay ever since he was a child. Although, as a child, he was molested by one of his foster mother's boyfriends, that wasn't the cause of him being like he was today.

Sweets grew up knowing that he was different than the other little knuckleheads that ran around his block, and it was apparent to everyone else that he had feminine characteristics. Kids his age taunted him daily, and it wasn't until he hit high school that he began to accept himself.

When he was in the tenth grade, Sweets met one of Flint's most notorious gangsters, Smitty Jake. Smitty was a smooth OG and a retired hustler, but he was still respected around the city. He was married with three children at home, but he still found time to mess around with men. His fascination with men, young and old, was what drew him to Sweets, and the two had a love affair that introduced Sweets to an entirely different perspective of the homosexual lifestyle.

Smitty would take Sweets out of town to gay underground clubs, where they would partake in all types of sexual acts. Looking at Smitty, one wouldn't know that he was gay, and even in his own eyes, he wasn't. He was married and had a family, which is how he justified his sexuality. "Gay men don't have wives and kids," he told himself. And anyone who ever said otherwise always came up missing.

Smitty was a killer, and hustling was second nature to him. He groomed Sweets into the young hustler that he was today. He once told Sweets, "You don't have to be a straight man to be a gangster. That's something that's just in you. Either you got it, or you don't. Either you built for the streets, or you ain't, simple as that. Don't hide who you are, Sweet Tooth."

Smitty was the one who had nicknamed Sweets in the first place, initially calling him Sweet Tooth. Sweets shortened the name himself.

"Do you, and stay true to yourself," Smitty told his young prodigy. "You blast on any nigga who got something to say about it. I've lived a double life for so long that I don't know which life is real. Don't be like me. Don't let another man's judgment dictate how you want to live your life."

Once Smitty uttered those words, Sweets ran with them. He came out of the closet, and any dude that talked that slick shit or tried to test him because of his sexual preference found himself six feet underneath the earth. *And if Jamaica Joe think he's any different,* Sweets thought, *I'll put the steel to his dome.*

Jamaica Joe called a meeting for all his workers and block lieutenants. He wanted to discuss the recent events with Sweets' crew and the beef that seemed to have taken itself to a whole 'nother level. Malek and Tariq, his two most trusted sol-

diers, stood next to him as he addressed the room-
ful of hustlers.

*How does this young nigga get to stand armored
guard at the front of the table? I been putting in work for
years and I just got to the front, ol' pretty-boy mu'fucka,*
Tariq thought. *I see this nigga is going to be a problem.
I should be running the Fifth Ward block, not this li'l
nigga.* Tariq discreetly gave Malek cold stares. He
hated the way that Joe took Malek under his wing
so quickly.

Honestly, Tariq wished that he and Joe had the
same relationship that Malek had with him. Jamaica Joe knew that Malek was a kingpin in the
making. Joe would always say, "You don't learn to
be a hustla. Hustlas are born." True indeed, Malek
was just that, a born hustla.

"We just gon' fall back for a minute," Joe said,
sitting at the head of the long red oak table.

One of the hustlers from Selby stood and said,
"Why haven't we clapped back yet? Sweets over there
feeling good about that caper he pulled. We've already been laying low for two weeks now. Let's get
at that nigga."

"We want him to start feeling himself. I'm playing
mental chess with that nigga," Joe replied. "You
have to know when to strike and when to fall back.
Once he start thinking that everything is all good,
then we get at his ass. Smell me? Sweets is over
there thinking that I'm just going to chalk it up as
a loss, but I got tricks for that nigga." Joe clenched
his fist. "Just when he thinks shit is sweet, we gon'
swoop on 'em." Joe tried to speak calmly, but they
could hear the anxiousness in his voice.

Malek just stood back and listened. He had been reaping the rewards of being down with Jamaica Joe's empire. Now it was time for him to prove himself and put in some real work. He never expected to be a street dude. Yeah, he was born and raised in the toughest hood in America, but he was always focusing on basketball. While his friends and teammates were falling victim to the allure of the streets, he knew that b-ball was his ticket out of the hood, so he did everything not to jeopardize it.

He had it all mapped out. He was positive that he would be drafted into the league, so he found a chick that was down for him early on in his high school career. Halleigh had been digging Malek way back in middle school, before there was even the thought of the NBA, which was why he chose her to be his girl. He didn't want some gold-diggin' chick to come along when he got rich; although since he and Halleigh never officially got together until tenth grade in high school, that's exactly what his mother thought she was.

What other people thought, including his mother, didn't change the way Malek felt about Halleigh, though. He wanted a "down chick" that he could spend his life with, and thought he'd found that in Halleigh. He'd planned on marrying her right after the draft, but life happened and interrupted all of his plans. Now instead of doing what he loved and making millions for it, he was doing what so many other dudes in Flint had died trying to do: achieve the American dream. Malek had moved up the ranks so quickly, he'd made mad enemies within his own camp already, some of whom he didn't even know about.

Joe pulled out his gun and laid it on the table. "Y'all ready to bring the heat to this mu'fucka?"

Malek nodded.

Tariq replied, "No doubt. That's what I do best."

Everyone in the room was in agreement, and the tension could be felt in the air.

"Good," Joe stated, "because blood is about to flow. Anybody who is caught associating with a South Side mu'fucka can get it. I don't care if the mu'fucka is your uncle, your cousin, or your got-damn daddy. Niggas gon' have to choose. Either you South Side or North Side. I got to show this nigga who he fuckin' with . . . and soon."

Chapter Fourteen

"I'll be back, Tash," Halleigh announced as she walked into Tasha's hotel room. "I'm about to run to the store. You want me to pick up some more condoms?"

Tasha, on the phone setting up a meeting for one of Mimi's johns, put her finger up to signal for Halleigh to hold on. "I told you we don't do that *pissing* shit," Tasha stated into the phone, a disgusted look on her face.

After a few seconds, she said, "All right, she's in room eight-ten. And we don't carry change, so have your shit correct." She hung up the phone and turned toward Halleigh. "Them white mu'-fuckas be on some freaky-ass shit." She laughed.

"Hell yeah." Halleigh giggled. She'd had her share of them, but if she knew Mimi, for an extra twenty spot, she was about to be drinking a full glass of water and then releasing it on her next john.

Tasha looked at Halleigh and noticed that her appearance still continued to deteriorate as each day passed. She looked tired and run-down, her eyes were red as if she hadn't slept in weeks, and her skin had lost its healthy, youthful glow.

Tasha reached into the nightstand near the bed and pulled out a ten dollar bill. "You been ripping and running to the store a lot lately. What? You trying to avoid making this money here? You know if you need a break, all you got to do is tell me. I'll find a way to cover for you with Manolo. I'd rather you take a break and get your shit together than get to the point where you can't make no money at all. Trust me, you don't want to see that day."

Halleigh yawned and rubbed her eyes. "Nah, I'm good, Tasha," she said, lying to Tasha and herself. "I don't even give a fuck anymore, you know. Once you've fucked one, you've fucked 'em all. I've accepted the fact that this is my life. Like you said, there is no way out. Besides, the same predicament that landed me here in the first place is the one that's keeping me here. I ain't got no other place to go."

Tasha frowned. She'd never heard Halleigh talk like that, and she was genuinely concerned. "Hal, girl, are you okay?" She had grown to care for her and Mimi as if they were her little sisters. Those were the only two Manolo Mamis she ever fraternized with.

"Like I said, I'm good." Halleigh held the door

open and waited for Tasha's response. "Anyway, do you need something from the store?"

Tasha extended her hand with the ten dollar bill in it. "Yeah, bring me back some condoms and a bag of hot Cheetos."

Halleigh took the money and put it in her pocket. She hurried through the hallway and caught the elevator down to the lobby. She was almost running, she was so eager to get to her destination.

She made her way to the alley up the street, where her new best friend was waiting for her.

"Hey, Li'l Rina." Scratch knew that Halleigh would be coming. She always visited him around the same time, and he always had the drug waiting for her. He pulled open the top flap on his cardboard box and offered her a seat in his very humble abode.

She watched eagerly as he pumped poison into his arms. "Hurry up, Scratch," she whined.

He closed his eyes as the drug took him to a state of pure bliss.

"Come on, quit hogging it." Halleigh scratched her forearm. She attempted to snatch the belt and needle from him.

"Come on now, Li'l Rina," Scratch said, pulling away. "I done told you that this ain't for you." Scratch repeated the same line he always repeated to Halleigh before he'd give in. "You too good for this. Look at yourself." He pointed to her. "You got your whole life ahead of you." Scratch was feeling guilty that he'd introduced her to the deadly habit, even though he saw to it that she got it on a regular, taking the cliché "misery loves company" to a whole new level.

"Look at you!" Halleigh snapped back. "You out here doing the same thing, so don't try to give me the you-better-than-this speech! Don't judge me. I'm tired of hearing that shit, Scratch. You need to live right yourself." She grabbed the belt violently from him.

"I'm an old man. My life is almost over anyway. I've lived, you haven't. You can still beat this."

Halleigh didn't even let her brain absorb the words. She disregarded him as she always did, grabbed the needle, and put it into her arm. Scratch shook his head, knowing she was going to do what she wanted to do, so he shut up about it before he blew his high arguing with her.

A few minutes later, Halleigh was so gone off her high, she forgot that she was supposed to be back at the hotel. She had messed around and stayed in the alley with Scratch for more than an hour.

Once the high began to wear down some, she came to her senses. "Gotta go, Scratch," she said quickly as she kissed Scratch on the cheek and then stood up. He was in the middle of a lean and didn't respond.

Halleigh jumped up and walked quickly back to the hotel. She ran into Tasha's room and announced, "I'm back," like she'd only been gone a hot second.

"Damn, Hal! It took your ass almost two hours to hit the corner store?" Tasha asked in irritation.

She had girls who couldn't take johns because she didn't have any condoms, so waiting on Halleigh to return had her missing money.

"The store on this street was closed. I had to go all out the way to find the next one."

Tasha held her hand out to Halleigh. "Well, where the condoms at?"

Halleigh just looked at her empty palm in confusion. *Damn! I did tell her I was gon' bring those back. I forgot all about that.* She didn't even have time to think of an excuse. "I forgot all about them, Tash. Sorry, girl. It slipped my mind."

Tasha said, "And my Cheetos?" her hand still extended. But from the look on Halleigh's face, it was evident that she'd forgotten those too. Tasha smacked her lips and dropped her hand.

Tasha frowned as she peeped Halleigh's demeanor. She was dazed and could barely keep her eyes open. Her words came out one on top of the other in a slurring fit. Tasha could see the signs clear as day, but she didn't want her assumption to be right. *She's been getting high. I know she ain't noddin'.*

Tasha didn't want to outright ask, so she took an indirect approach. "Well, what you get?"

"Damn! What is this? An interrogation? I told you I forgot your shit! I ate my shit up before I came back!" she yelled.

"Look, Ms. Halleigh, you need to calm the fuck down. You ain't foolin' nobody. I've been around the block more times than you can count. I know you out there." She looked Halleigh up and down. "And from the looks of it, you out there bad."

Halleigh rolled her eyes up in her head, trying to keep tears from falling out of them.

"Look, Hal, you getting high ain't gon' solve your problems. And I'm not trying to ride you. I'm just looking out for you, girl. That shit ain't no good. Trust me. I've seen that monkey beat the best."

Halleigh heard what Tasha was saying, but she wasn't trying to. As far as she was concerned, all Tasha wanted to do was make sure Halleigh didn't get so far gone that she couldn't make any more money. "I'm straight, Tasha," Halleigh told her, "so just get off my back. I'm a grown-ass woman. You may not think so, but from the first time I opened my legs for Manolo's lying ass, I grew up, so I can handle my shit just fine." A single tear managed to escape Halleigh's eyes, but she quickly and force-fully knocked it away, practically smacking herself in the face.

It hurt Tasha's heart to see Halleigh go out like so many other young girls had done. There used to be thirteen Manolo Mamis, but three had been lost to their drug addiction. Loita died as a result of an overdose. That's why Tasha always made it a point not to get close with any of the girls. Tasha and Loita, the half-Hispanic–half-white girl who used to pull in over a thousand dollars a night, had been tight like the fist on an Afro pick. Men used to love her exotic look, calling up and requesting her specifically, sometimes booking her a full weekend in advance.

Tasha loved Loita's honesty and loyalty to the

game. Dudes would tip her twenty, fifty, sometimes a hundred dollars, and she would always turn it in to Tasha, along with her regular earnings. But Tasha always let her keep it, to reward her honesty. In turn, Loita would always throw Tasha half of the tip for her pocket. The two looked out for each other. That's just how it was between them.

And even though Loita ran circles around the other girls when it came to checking in loot, she had no enemies. No one was jealous or envious of her because she had such a beautiful spirit. There was nothing to hate.

If another girl came up short on dough or didn't make enough money to please Manolo, Loita was known, on occasion, to give her tip money to make the difference. She just got down like that, and the same couldn't be said for any other girl in the crew.

But when Loita started going MIA after a gig with a regular, Tasha sensed something was wrong. Turned out, the john got her hooked on heroin and started to pay Loita for her services with drugs instead of cash. Her appearance started to deteriorate, and so did her loyalty. She stopped checking in tips to Tasha, and just like Halleigh was doing now, spent more time at the corner store than in the hotel room.

The signs were there, but Tasha never stepped up and spoke on it. She wished she had, especially the night she had to go get the hotel manager to open Loita's hotel room door after not hearing from her, only to find her laying dead on the bed, a needle in her arm.

Tasha couldn't let the same thing happen to

Halleigh, not under her watch. "Why are you doing this to yourself, Halleigh?" she asked.

"Why else? Because I have to. It's the only way I know how to do this thing. It's the only way I can keep laying on my back every day and let you send ten different niggas in my hotel room to fuck me."

This was the boldest Halleigh had ever been with Tasha, but she was on an emotional overload right now.

"I'm only nineteen, Tash, and I'm on the track for Manolo. All I wanted was to be with my man, you know." Tears rolled down Halleigh's face. "Malek means everything to me, but because of Manolo, I can't be with him. Do you know how it feels? Not being able to be with someone who your heart just burns for?" Halleigh wiped her nose with the back of her hand. "I have to get high to get by, and that's my business, not yours. Your business is making sure I turn all my money over to you." Halleigh was throwing a guilt trip on Tasha so Tasha would feel her pain.

"You in my face day and night, acting like you care, but you don't. All you care about is how many niggas I suck and fuck. That's how it has always been, and that's how it's always going to be, so squash the act about you being all concerned about me and shit," she screamed. Halleigh was upset with the world and was letting the heroin speak for her. She knew that Tasha had grown quite close to her, but she didn't care. She needed to vent, so she continued with her rant. "No, you aren't the one who put me on the ho stroll, but you're the one who helped him get in my head. So don't be trying to act all innocent, like you didn't have shit to do with it."

Halleigh wiped every last teardrop away. Hell, she was tired of crying. She had no more tears left. Her sadness had transformed into resentment and hatred, and she was taking it all out on Tasha.

Halleigh attempted to leave the room, but Tasha jumped up and blocked the doorway. "No, Halleigh, wait!" Tasha begged. She knew that Halleigh was telling the truth. She did help Manolo manipulate his young girls, but this time she wished she hadn't participated. Halleigh was too pure for what Manolo had in store for her, and Tasha knew that almost from the first time she'd set eyes on her. Halleigh couldn't handle the game, and Tasha felt obligated to get the monkey off her back, especially since she had participated in the cause that put the monkey there in the first place.

"Just calm down, sweetheart," Tasha said, holding her hands up in surrender. "You know that I would never intentionally hurt you. You are like my sister." Tasha choked up, her eyes filled with tears. She imagined saying the same thing to Loita. If she had, maybe Loita would still be alive today. "I know this lifestyle ain't healthy for you. If I can get you to Malek, will you promise me you will stay off the drugs?"

Halleigh couldn't believe her ears. Had Tasha just made her the offer she thought she heard?

"Okay, Hal?" Tasha placed a hand on either side of Halleigh's face.

Halleigh nodded her head. "Yes," she replied, sounding like a hopeful child. "Tasha, I swear I will. I swear to God. Just get me to Malek. Get me out of this life. Help me. Please help me."

Tasha hugged Halleigh tightly, looked up toward the ceiling and said a short prayer. *Please help me with this, God. I don't know how I'm gon' do it, but I have to help her out of this.* It was the first time that Tasha had prayed since she was a child. She just hoped God was listening.

Tasha pulled away from Halleigh and put her hands on her shoulders. "Listen, stay here. I'll be back in a while. Do not leave this room, Hal. If the phone rings, just answer it and direct the traffic to the other girls. You got that?"

Halleigh nodded.

"Good. I'll be back," Tasha said as she exited the room.

After Tasha closed the door behind her, she stood there with her back against it, still holding the knob. She exhaled. Because Halleigh was a genuinely good person, Tasha's heart ached for her. Tasha knew that she was partly to blame for Halleigh's disposition. Being the madam of the house, it was her job to make the girls feel as if they had nowhere else to go. The situation with Halleigh had gone too far, however, with her resorting to heroin as an escape, just like Loita.

I have to find Malek for her.

Tasha knew there was a possibility that Manolo would harm Halleigh if he ever found out that she reunited with Malek, but she knew for sure that drugs would kill her. Tasha couldn't just sit back and watch her girl send herself into an early grave. So she had a job to do. She had made a promise that she intended to keep.

And so she released the doorknob and began her trek in search of Malek.

Chapter Fifteen

Tasha pulled her car up to Joe's home on Cold-water and turned off her ignition. She was down with Sweets, Manolo, and the South Side, but she was also well known throughout the entire city. She and Joe had enjoyed some mind-blowing nights to-gether a couple years ago, and she was confident that she was safe on his side of town.

She stared up at his four-bedroom home and butterflies entered her stomach. She wasn't afraid of Jamaica Joe, but she was afraid of what Manolo would do to her if he ever found out that she was in the presence of his enemy.

She pulled down the sun visor and looked at herself in the mirror attached to it. She checked her M•A•C makeup to make sure her shit was tight, and then she stepped out of the car, gracing the cold Flint streets with her Jimmy Choo stilet-tos. Most hoes in Flint didn't even know what the hell Jimmy Choo was. It was more like, "Jimmy who?"

These whack chicks probably thinking it's a new Chinese joint or something, no-class-having-ass bitches, Tasha thought arrogantly as she adjusted the strap on her shoe and then made her way to Joe's front porch.

Tasha was a top-notch ho, and she knew it. And so did everybody who knew her. She kept up with all the latest fashions. If she'd been born in a big city, her dreams of becoming a model might have been realistic, but in a small city like Flint, it just wasn't happening. As she walked up to Joe's, she quickly caught the attention of the group of men posted around his back entryway. They lusted blatantly, commenting on her five-foot–nine-inch stature, slim waist, and wide hips. Her calf muscles were defined from years of walking up and down Flint's tracks, and her perky C cups set her figure off just right. Tasha was damn near perfect.

The only thing she didn't like about herself were the scars on her back, left by the last john she'd serviced. The psycho had almost taken her life when he became upset that he had to pay extra money for some extra acts that Tasha had performed for him. He ended up pulling a box cutter on her, eventually getting the extra acts he wanted, cutting her and taking them by force. She fought back with every ounce of strength she had in her, ignoring the burning stings from the blade. She was lucky to leave with her life, and after the incident, she convinced Manolo to put her on as the madam of the house.

Tasha adjusted her bra strap and licked her lips. She didn't mind at all the slick comments that Joe's associates made as she stood before them. She was used to lame niggas spitting whack lines to get down. Little did they know, if they started talking the right amount of money, they could have her. *Broke niggas don't never want to put their money where their mouth is.*

She came right out and said, "I'm looking for Malek. Does anybody know where I can find him?" She stood at the bottom of the porch steps, glancing from one dude to the next, waiting on a reply.

One of the guys said, "Damn, this li'l mu'fucka got bad bitches like you checking for him?"

Tasha ignored the comment.

One of the other men tapped lightly on the door and yelled through the screen, "Yo, Joe, tell Malek he got a bad bitch looking for him out here."

Jamaica Joe came to the screen and peered out. He instantly recognized Tasha. "Aw shit, Tash! Come on in," he stated, happy to see her.

As soon as she walked through the door, he embraced her. He looked over his shoulders and nodded for his guys to go check out shit, to make sure she didn't bring anybody else with her who might be trying to set him up.

"How you been doing, Joe?" Tasha tried to pull away from Joe's embrace, but was unable to, as he caressed her like a long-lost friend, feeling her up. "Look, Joe, you can stop it with the body search. I ain't got nothin' on me. I ain't come bringing no shit. I'm just looking for somebody, one of your homeboys, all right?"

Joe eased up and released her. He knew Tasha was good peoples, but with some of the shit going down lately, he could never be too sure. For all he knew, Manolo and Sweets had sent her to catch a nigga slippin' again.

"All right. You good, ma." He looked her up and down. "And still lookin' good too. By the way, how's that chump nigga treating you? You still running the Manolo Mamis, right?"

"I'm good, Joe."

"Yeah, that's what your mouth say. I don't know why you still in that game anyway. You know if you ever need something—"

"I'm good," she answered again.

Joe and Tasha had a nice little rapport going on between them. They always had, despite the beef between the two rival gangs. Joe had tried to pull her from underneath Manolo plenty of times, but Tasha wasn't trying to be the atomic bomb in a war that was already explosive enough. She knew the game, and she knew her place. Loyalty was important to her, even though she did enjoy spending time with Joe.

"Okay, okay. You killing me, though, coming to my spot, looking for my boy." Joe placed a hand on his heart, as if he'd been shot there.

His charming smile made Tasha laugh. "Come on now," she said. "You know me better than that. I need to talk to your boy about my girl Halleigh."

Before Jamaica Joe could respond, Malek walked into the room.

"Speak of the devil," Joe said.

Tasha stared up at the tall, handsome young boy

who stood before her. He was far from a boy, though. The nineteen-year-old was nice, with a body that had Tasha's eyes wandering. *Damn, this is why Hal's head is so gone off of him.* Tasha had to admit, with his charming features, she could see how Halleigh could fall in love with him.

"What about Halleigh?" Malek asked. Hearing her name had piqued his interest.

Tasha could sense the concern and anxiety in his voice and thought that it might be easier than she expected to hook them up. "She needs you," Tasha said simply. "Your girl is on some other shit right now. I don't want to put her business out like that, so I'm just gon' say it's bad. You're the only person she talks about. She is going crazy without you," Tasha stated in a serious tone. "Maybe you can talk some sense into her, 'cause as of now, she ain't trying to hear me."

Jamaica Joe interjected, "I know y'all ain't talking about that little trick from the party. Manolo's ho."

Tasha nodded, never taking her eyes off Malek.

"Yo, fuck that shit right now." Jamaica Joe put his hand on Malek's shoulder. The last thing he wanted was for Malek's head to be far gone on some broad while they had bigger things to tend to. He needed his soldier focused on the real business at hand—catching Sweets and his crew slipping.

Jamaica Joe had seen how fucked up Malek was after Halleigh chose Manolo over him the night of the party. His pain was evident from the look in his eyes, but as far as Joe was concerned, his business took priority over Malek's business with some high school girlfriend.

"That's Manolo's pussy, man," Joe said to Malek then turned his attention to Tasha. "She straight ho'ed my boy for that nigga. She deserves to be where she's at."

Tasha yelled when she saw Malek's expression turn cold. "Joe, it's not like that. You know how Manolo can get in these girls' heads. He told her that he would kill her *and* Malek."

"Nah. He can touch her, but this nigga right here can't be touched." Joe patted Malek on the shoulder, letting him know he had his back.

"Malek?" Tasha asked, her voice pleading with him to help Halleigh.

Jamaica Joe stared intently at him to see what his decision would be. He'd already made it clear that there was no riding the fence anymore. Malek had to choose. He was either North or South.

The light of hope Tasha had initially seen in Malek was now dimming. "Just come see her," Tasha said. "Please . . . that's all I'm asking."

Malek hesitated. The thought of Halleigh being in trouble bothered him, but he couldn't get past the fact that she'd put another nigga before him.

Joe got in his ear. "What's it gonna be, homie, North or South?" His tone was laced with a discreet warning that Malek better make the right choice or he might not even make it out of that house alive to go talk to Halleigh.

Malek looked up at Joe, even though he was replying to Tasha, and said, "I don't fuck with no South Side bitch." Then he walked away.

A smirk appeared on Joe's face. He nodded his head, pleased that Malek had made the right decision—money over bitches—and watched his boy walk away.

"Joe?" Tasha said as she looked his way for help.

Joe shrugged. *I know this ho don't think I'ma talk my boy into choosing her crew over mine.*

"Come on, Joe. Go talk to him."

"He a grown-ass man. That's his business."

"Yeah, but this is a matter of life and death. You have no idea how far gone this chick is. I ain't asking him to disregard his loyalty to you. I just want him to have one lousy gotdamn conversation with her. A conversation that could possibly save her life."

Joe simply shrugged again and then kissed Tasha on the cheek, letting her know it was still good between them.

Tasha sighed and threw her hands up in despair. She stormed out of the house. It was the first time in a long time that she felt like crying. *What do I tell this girl? I can't just walk in there and say, "He don't want your ass no more."*

Tasha drove slowly back to the hotel, trying to decide if she should lie to Halleigh and say that she couldn't find Malek but would keep trying. Perhaps that would buy her some time.

When Tasha got back to the hotel, she wasn't even in the room more than a few seconds before Halleigh jumped up, eager to find out if she'd tracked down Malek.

"Hey, Tash," Halleigh said excitedly. She kept peering behind Tasha, hoping Malek would walk through the door. "Where is he? What did he say?"

Tasha shook her head, but she was unable to form the words.

"Well, come on, tell me. Since when have you ever been at a loss for words?" Halleigh said, trying to keep the mood light. Tasha's mood was a sure sign that her attempt was unsuccessful. "You didn't find him, did you?"

At that moment, Tasha could have easily lied to Halleigh. She could have been persistent and kept going back at Malek until he gave in and talked to Halleigh; even if she had to throw some pussy at him just to get him to do it. But instead, the truth prevailed. "No, I found him."

There was a pregnant silence.

"And?" Halleigh finally said.

Tasha looked up with her saddened eyes.

"And he's not coming, is he?"

Before Tasha could even speak, Halleigh's excitement had turned to complete despair. She could only imagine what Malek said to Tasha. "He doesn't love me anymore." Halleigh fell weakly to her knees.

The sound that erupted from her body was enough to bring Tasha to tears as she fell to the floor with her friend and held her tightly. Despite what Halleigh thought, Tasha really did care about her; although at first, when Mimi brought her to the house to become a Manolo Mami, Tasha had a hint of jealousy in her bones for the young girl. She saw something in Halleigh, that "it" factor people sometimes talked about, and she didn't want "it" to take her place. But once Tasha realized that Halleigh wasn't a threat and that her only mission in life was to reunite with her boyfriend, Tasha quickly killed the jealous voice in her head. Now she had nothing but love for the young doe who had gotten herself caught in headlights.

"It's okay. It's going to be okay," Tasha repeated over and over in her attempt to comfort Halleigh.

Her words fell on deaf ears, though. Halleigh couldn't stop the pain she was feeling. She just sat on the floor hopelessly and cried enough tears to cleanse the entire city.

Tasha stroked Halleigh's hair and thought about her next move.

Chapter Sixteen

"Tasha, I don't know about y'all living at the hotel. That would be double the cost just for the rooms. Instead of paying for the rooms for a couple of hours, I would be paying full price," Manolo said, skepticism in his voice.

"Come on, Daddy. Think about it. We are missing out on so much money. By us being here at the hotel twenty-four hours, we could make twice as much money. It's a win-win situation," Tasha said convincingly as she talked into the phone in her hotel room. She hoped that Manolo would fall for the little trick she had up her sleeve, because she knew that she would need time to get Halleigh back right. If Manolo saw her in the state she was in, his method of detox would probably be another two weeks in the basement.

Manolo listened closely on the other end of the phone, while one of the girls filed his fingernails for him. Fortunately for Tasha, the more she talked, the more he began to see things her way. The mention of making more money had him game.

"All right, Tasha, but if the cash flow don't double up, I'ma take it out on that ass, hear me?" Manolo said sternly.

"Yeah, Daddy, I hear you. I'ma make you proud." With that, Tasha hung up the phone and focused her attention over to her bed. She knew the other girls weren't going to take too kindly to the new arrangement she'd just made with Manolo, but if she had to sacrifice their time and happiness to save one, then her mind was made up: she was going to do it.

Tasha knew that she had bought herself some time. She wanted to keep Manolo away from Halleigh for as long as possible, until she got better. Seeing her would be a dead giveaway. He would easily see that Halleigh was fiending for one of two things: either dope or Malek. And neither one would please him.

Now that Tasha had taken care of phase one of the plan with Manolo, it was time to take care of phase two with Halleigh. She went into one of the dominatrix bags that the girls sometimes used on their customers. She then made her way over to Halleigh, who was coming out of a dope coma.

"Let me go, you crazy bitch!" Halleigh yelled as she tried to avoid being handcuffed to the bed. She was too weak to stand a chance against Tasha.

"Look, Halleigh, I'm sorry about this. I don't want to have to leave you tied up like this, but I can't sit here and watch you continue to hurt yourself. You are killing yourself slowly on that needle. Believe me, I've seen that shit destroy some of the toughest chicks. Let me help you, okay?" Tasha said in a comforting tone. She looked into Halleigh's baggy eyes and felt sorry for her. Determined to help Halleigh shake her habit, she wasn't about to let the streets swallow her whole like they did Loita.

"Bitch, I said let me go!" Halleigh screamed as she continued to squirm and jerk to no avail.

Tasha had to head out and take care of some business, and she didn't want Halleigh to hit the streets looking for another fix. Unfortunately, part of her plan meant that she herself would have to come out of retirement and hit the track to compensate for Halleigh. While out tricking, she knew she had to keep Halleigh restrained, or else the first thing she'd do was go out and get a hit.

"I will let you go, Hal, but you have to kick this shit first. I'm so sorry, but it's for your own good." Tasha looked at her, hoping that Halleigh could see in her eyes how sincere she was about helping her.

"Aghh! Aghh! Help me!" Halleigh screamed, hoping her cries for help would grab someone's attention.

Tasha let her scream, knowing that no one would come and check on her. They were at a "whore motel," and screaming and begging was a common sound coming from their rooms.

"Go ahead and scream all you like," Tasha told her, "but I'm not going to let you go until I get back. I know you don't believe me when I say it, but I really do care about you and what happens to you. I don't want to see you end up like . . ." Tasha's words trailed off. "Look, I love you, girl, and I know that you are going to beat this shit." Tasha sat on the bed next to Halleigh and began to rub her head.

"I don't need your help!" Halleigh forcefully yanked away from Tasha. "I need a hit!"

"That shit is going to kill you, Halleigh," Tasha yelled as she looked down at her with tears in her eyes. Why couldn't Halleigh see that all she was trying to do was help her? Tasha could have easily just let her fall off and become like some of the other girls, but she wouldn't be able to live with herself. She just couldn't understand why Halleigh wouldn't want the help somebody was trying to offer her.

"Maybe I want to die, Tasha. You ever thought about that? Malek doesn't want me. What man would? There's no point in living," she said, staring at the ceiling.

"Fuck him, Halleigh, and anybody else, for that matter." She grabbed Halleigh by the face. "Do this for you! Don't end up like your mother. Fight this."

Halleigh was offended that Tasha would even insinuate that she was anything like her mother. "I'm not going to end up like my mother. I'm nothing like that bitch."

Tasha realized that she'd hit a nerve, and so she decided to go for the jugular. She let out a menacing chuckle. "Huh? Nothing like her? Have you looked in the mirror lately? You're just like her. Matter of fact . . ."—Tasha got up and went over to her purse, pulled out a M•A•C makeup compact, opened it up and held the mirror in front of Halleigh—"See. Look at yourself. Just look at you."

Halleigh turned. She didn't want to see herself. She could only imagine what her reflection looked like. "Stop it! No!" Halleigh continued to struggle.

Tasha grabbed her tightly by the chin to hold her face steady and rammed the mirror in front of her. "I said look! Look at you. If you're not your mother, then who are you?"

Halleigh began to weep, but it didn't stop Tasha from making her point. "Who are you then?"

When Halleigh's eyes met those looking back at her in the mirror, she shut them tight and began to cry. "I don't know," she finally answered. "I don't know who I am anymore. Oh, God," she cried with heaving shoulders.

Tasha uttered a sigh of relief, figuring she'd made her point and that Halleigh had had enough. Tasha took Halleigh into her arms and rocked her.

Just then, a thought came into Halleigh's mind. "I hear what you're saying, Tasha,"—She rattled the handcuffs—"about me being locked down and all, but what will Manolo say? He'll know that I'm fucked up when he sees that I'm not bringing in any money. I'm better off killing myself with drugs anyway after he gets a hold of me."

But Tasha knew that was just a last-ditch drug addict tactic to convince her to let Halleigh go.

Halleigh was right about Manolo's cash, though. If he sensed that the money was coming short, he would definitely put a foot in their asses. That's why Tasha decided to come out of retirement. She didn't want to go back to ho'ing, but she knew that she had to, to keep Halleigh's condition a secret from Manolo. She'd promised herself that she would never turn a trick again, but desperate times called for desperate measures. And this was definitely one of those times. Halleigh was like a little sister to her, and she refused to let her continue down the path she was taking.

You have to make this game your hustle, not your life. Tricks get in this game for the wrong reasons.

Tasha released Halleigh and then stood up to head for the door. "I've taken care of that." She opened the compact she already had in her hands and touched up her face with the powder puff.

Tasha knew being a prostitute wasn't easy. It was best to get money and then get out because in this game, if you stay in it too long, it becomes you. And when the streets become you, there is no turning back.

Tasha had on her four-inch stilettos and a black miniskirt. Before walking out the door, she walked over to the dresser mirror to apply some mascara. She could hear Halleigh moaning in the background in obvious pain, and she wanted so badly to uncuff her, but that would only be enabling her friend to go and do more drugs.

"Sorry, Hal," Tasha whispered as Halleigh continued to moan loudly, "but this is for your own good." Tasha finished applying her mascara then headed for the door.

"Please help me, Tasha. I hurt so badly," Halleigh said, tears streaming down her face. Her body was craving the drug, and sharp pains shot through her stomach as the monkey jumped on her back.

It's for her own good. Tasha exited the room. Somebody had to fill in for Halleigh, and Tasha was taking one for the team.

"Please! Please, Tash, help me out. I need a fix. I swear this will be the last time," Halleigh begged.

Tasha knew that if she looked back at Halleigh, she would give in, so she just exited the room with tears in her eyes and never looked back.

Chapter Seventeen

"You like that, Daddy?" Tasha asked the john seductively as she massaged his balls with one hand and gripped his pipe with the other. Tasha peeked up at the man, and he was in pure bliss. He was about to cum, and she hadn't even put her mouth on his dick yet. This is what she called "easy money." As she continued to massage his balls and blow on his manhood, she felt his legs stiffen up. She gave him one good stroke and licked his head, and that was it. Game over.

Tasha hadn't lost her touch. She made that fool cum in under a minute. She wasn't the best for nothing.

"That's a hundred and fifty dollars, Daddy." Tasha got off her knees and held out her palm. She had charged him for a head job, when in actuality he only got jerked off. The fool was so in love, he didn't know the difference. Tasha could peep vulnerable men from a mile away. The way he was moaning and looking into Tasha's eyes, she knew from jump that she could overcharge him.

The man handed Tasha two crisp hundred dollar bills. "Keep the change."

Tasha got the money and then hopped out of his two-door Cadillac. She walked the track, trying to pick up her next john. She had only been on the ho stroll for a couple of hours, and she almost had six hundred dollars, just that quick. As luck would have it, she ran into one of her better customers, who was more than happy to see her back on the grind.

Tasha was a veteran. She knew which johns to service and which johns not to. If a john didn't look like he was spending big dough, she passed on him. For her, being out there all night fucking with small-timers just wasn't worth it.

Tasha grew hungry and stopped at the chicken spot on the corner of Clio and Stewart to grab a bite to eat and to use their bathroom to freshen up a little. She picked up two chicken dinners then walked out of the spot.

"Hey, miss."

She turned and saw the store owner coming her way. He was the one who had just waited on her.

Once he finally caught up with her, he said, "You uh, you uh, forgot your change." The way he said it was kind of peculiar, and he seemed to be looking around to make sure no one was watching him.

"Oh, did I?" Tasha could have sworn that he'd given it to her.

She started to check her purse, but then he extended his hand to her. Inside of it was a hundred dollar bill.

Tasha took it out of his hand and looked at it like it was nothing but a dollar bill. "And what's this for?"

"Oh, yeah, I, uh, just was wondering if you could do something for me."

Once again, Tasha looked at the hundred dollar bill like it was nothing.

The man continued. "I was just, uh, wondering if you could come with me to my truck. It's, uh, right over there."

Tasha's eyes followed his finger to the black SUV with tinted windows. "And?"

"And just watch me."

A puzzled look came across Tasha's face. Seeing her confusion, the man went on. "And just watch me, you know, take care of my business."

"Ohhh," Tasha said, nodding her head. She smiled and then licked her lips. Once again, a vulnerable one. She loved how she attracted his kind. She knew that she could have easily manipulated him out of more money if she threw in a couple of extra treats, but to watch him jerk off for a bill was good enough. Besides, she didn't want her food to get cold, so she obliged him, joining him over in his truck and watching him, while he watched her watch him jerk off.

Three minutes tops was all it took. Now that was easy money!

Tasha's feet were killing her as she headed back to the hotel. She hadn't strolled in stilettos in almost two years and was paying the price.

When Tasha made it to the room, her heart dropped when she opened the door. Halleigh was gone. She'd found a way to slither out of the handcuffs. Tasha flopped on the bed and buried her face in her hands, knowing that she'd failed Halleigh.

A noise from the bathroom startled Tasha, and she quickly looked in the direction of the commotion. She walked to the bathroom and opened the door to find Halleigh with her head over the toilet bowl.

"Halleigh, are you okay, girl?" Tasha dropped to her knees and pulled Halleigh's hair away from her face. Halleigh looked horrible, like she had lost even more weight within the past couple of hours. Her body was soaking wet because of all of the sweating she was doing. Halleigh trembled as a chill ran through her body.

"I stayed in the room. I didn't go anywhere. I didn't go," Halleigh said in a child-like, whiny voice. "See? You can trust me."

"I know, baby, I know." Tasha continued to rub her hair. She understood that Halleigh was actually trying to beat her addiction because she didn't leave the room when she had a chance.

"Come on, girl." Tasha helped Halleigh up and began to pull off her sweaty clothes.

Tasha helped her into the shower and let the water hit her face and body. She stood right by her side, washing her and holding her up. Halleigh's body was so weak. The dependence on the drug had gotten the best of her.

She's so young. I can barely handle this life and I'm twenty-four, Tasha thought.

Tasha had been involved in the pimp game for years. Just seeing Halleigh in this position and being reminded of Loita, whom she herself had introduced to the game, Tasha decided that she couldn't do this anymore. It was time for a change. The first chance she got, she would come up with a plan to do something better with her life. When she did finally decide to make the move, she promised herself that she would take Halleigh with her.

Chapter Eighteen

Halleigh's eyes darted frantically around the room as she tried to gather her bearings. She felt like she was dying. Her body hurt so badly, and no matter what she did, nothing eased the pain. She couldn't believe that her life had gotten so bad in such a short period of time, and she was ashamed of herself for losing control. All of those years she'd watched her mother's condition deteriorate because of drugs. Now she was following in her footsteps. What would Malek think if he saw her now?

Halleigh's body shook violently as the draft in the room sent cold shivers up her spine. She was freezing, and nothing she did could warm her body. She broke out in constant cold sweats as she squirmed and wrapped herself with the covers on the bed. The slightest touch hurt her skin, and she felt like the sun was burning out her eyes every time she attempted to open them.

She'd been trying to kick her habit for weeks, and it just didn't seem to be working. The only time she could ever seem to pull herself together was when Tasha warned her that Manolo might be dropping by. Of course, Tasha always told him that Halleigh was with a john, but how much longer would that little stunt of theirs work before he started getting suspicious?

Just last week, when Manolo dropped by the hotel to check things out, Tasha was sure her little plan was about to be discovered. It was the motel keeper who almost made the plan backfire. The skinny, gray-haired man, his skin the color of coffee with a hint of cream, said to Manolo when he saw him entering the motel and heading over to the elevators, "Business picking up, I see."

Manolo simply nodded. He wasn't into talking about his business with strangers. As far as he was concerned, old dude could have recently been bought by the feds to try to trap him, or something. But on second thought, Manolo knew that if anything was in the works, his hired cop, Troy, would have tipped him off. After all, that's why Troy got his pick of the litter of free pussy from the Manolo Mamis, plus a little green on the side.

Right before the elevator door opened to welcome Manolo's presence, the motel keeper added, "Yeah, when your girl came down a few weeks ago and added another room to your already-set block of five, I knew things must be picking up for you."

Manolo had already gotten inside the elevator

and the doors were about to close, but hearing the man's last comment, he held his hand out, stopping the doors. "What did you say?" Manolo inquired. "Another room?"

"Well, yeah," the clerk said with a tone and expression on his face that said maybe he had spoken on something that he shouldn't have. "You, uh, have the six rooms now, right?"

When Manolo's facial expression clearly showed that he knew nothing about adding another room to their block of five, the clerk tried to clean things up. After all, he didn't want to mess up his money by spilling the beans on something he shouldn't have. "Maybe I made a mistake."

"Nah," Manolo said. "You don't look like the type of fella who makes mistakes. But just to be sure, why don't you double-check your records?"

"Uh, well, uh, yes, sir," the man stammered as he shuffled through some paperwork and receipts. After resting on one piece of paper in particular, he held it up and said, "You're right. I didn't make a mistake. Six rooms as of last month."

Fire shot out of Manolo's nostrils as he snatched the paper from the man and read the receipt that showed Tasha had been paying for an extra room. *What the fuck is going on, and why is my money being spent on shit without my prior consent?*

He had agreed with Tasha as far as paying for the rooms twenty-four/seven, but she hadn't said anything about adding an extra room to the block. Tasha, he was sure, never made mistakes. That's why she held the rank with him that she did. So he was almost one hundred percent certain that this wasn't an oversight on her part, but deliberate deception instead. But why? Why would Tasha decide to play him after all these years? Not once was the money ever short. She'd never beat him for one red cent, and now here she was trying to do something extra on the side without his knowledge. He expected this type of thing from Mimi, but not Tasha.

Is she trying to start up her own thing on the side, steal my business?

If she was, she wouldn't have been the first. The madam Manolo had before Tasha tried to pull that exact same stunt. All the while she was supposed to be minding the Manolo Mami business, she was minding her own on the side, forming a prostitution ring so that once she slipped out from under Manolo, she would already have her own thing set up.

Of course, that didn't sit too well with Manolo, and unfortunately for her—but fortunate for Tasha—the woman went missing right on time for Tasha to take her spot in Manolo's ring. But if Tasha called herself doing the same thing, who would he get to replace her when she went missing?

With the paper in hand, Manolo turned back toward the elevator with every intention of going to confront Tasha with this newfound information. But as he stood there waiting on the elevator, he had a second thought. He wouldn't outright confront her just yet. Instead, he would test her and watch her, to see if anything seemed out of the ordinary with her. He didn't want to believe that Tasha would try to double-cross him. Hell, even Tina Turner stuck it out with Ike, and Manolo treated

Tasha way better than Ike treated Tina. But if he'd learned anything about putting his trust in someone, it was not to—no exceptions.

Manolo simply folded the paper, placed it in his pocket and got on the elevator, heading up to check in with Tasha, to make sure it was business as usual. And for her sake, it better be.

Tasha had just returned from trickin' with a john when Manolo entered the hotel room. "Oh shit!" she exclaimed.

"What's the matter, baby girl? Did I scare you?" Manolo walked over to her, grabbed her by the back of her hair, and stared her in the eyes.

She tried her best not to tremble. "What?" she asked Manolo, wondering why he was just standing there looking down at her like she'd stolen something from him.

Manolo didn't speak. He just tightened his grip and then proceeded to ram his tongue down her throat.

Tasha wanted to throw up. Manolo's touch used to reassure her of her role in his life, but now it only sickened her. Besides, if he only knew what she'd just done with that tongue of hers, he'd reconsider sticking his in her mouth.

After tonguing Tasha down for a few seconds, Manolo pulled her away from him and stared in her eyes again.

"What, Daddy? What is it?"

Manolo just stood there searching her eyes. Usually, if someone was deceiving him, their eyes were a dead giveaway, but when he looked at Tasha, he saw the same thing that he always saw in her eyes—loyalty. "Nothing," Manolo finally replied. "I just missed you, is all."

Tasha relaxed a little. For a minute there, she was afraid that Manolo might have heard something about her from the street. But she showed no fear as she maintained her composure. "I missed you too." Tasha pulled away from Manolo and headed toward the bathroom.

"Where you going?" Manolo looked her up and down. He noticed that she was a little bit more dressed up than usual.

"Uh, just to the bathroom. I just got back from walking to the store. I didn't know you were stopping by."

"Well, aren't you a little overdressed for the store?"

"You know when I step out I always gotta do it right. After all, I'm a walking advertisement for the Manolo Mamis. Niggas see me, and like stray little puppies, they wanna follow me home. And home is where the money is," Tasha said, thinking quick on her feet.

She walked back over toward Manolo and said seductively, "Anyway, like I was saying, I didn't know you were stopping by. Otherwise, I wouldn't have gotten myself all sweaty and stuff down there. I would have kept it crisp for you." She ran her fingers across Manolo's lips. "You know, with me running this spot twenty-four hours now, I never get to see you as often, and a girl has needs too, Daddy. And I know you ain't gon' leave me hanging. You gotta hit me off with a little something because

God knows when I'll get the chance to be alone with you again."

Manolo closed his eyes and moaned as Tasha cupped his manhood and began to massage it.

"Oh shit, baby. You know Daddy wouldn't do you like that."

"Good." Tasha backed away from him slowly and sensually toward the bathroom. "Then you stay right there. Promise me you won't leave me, Daddy," Tasha begged.

"Promise." Manolo watched her disappear behind the bathroom door. "Mm-mm-mm," he said to himself. He began to undress, and reasonable doubt regarding Tasha's loyalty to him slowly began to vacate his mind. *Maybe business was booming, and she had to get an extra room and just didn't worry about telling me, since it's not going to be a regular thing. Yeah, that's probably it.*

Manolo lay down on the bed, caressing his manhood and waiting on Daddy's favorite little girl to come please him. *Hell, even if she's up to no good after all, I don't see no reason why I can't get one last fuck-and-suck before I see to it that she or anyone who decides to jump camp with her, like Toni Braxton said, never breathes again.*

Chapter Nineteen

As Halleigh lay there in pain, she didn't know what to do. "God, help me," she moaned, grabbing her stomach. She lifted herself up and tried to crawl out of the hotel bed, but ended up landing on her knees beside the bed. She remained in that spot as if her knees were magnetized to the floor.

A few weeks ago, after convincing Manolo to allow the girls to run business twenty-four/seven in the motel, Tasha had gone down and paid the clerk for an extra room to house Halleigh. She didn't want any of the other girls getting wind that Halleigh wasn't putting in any work at all. That alone would've given them cause to run back and start complaining to Manolo. So Tasha just got Halleigh her own room, away from the ones where the other girls tricked, so that she could get better.

Tasha even used her own money to pay for the

room. In all the years she'd dealt with Manolo, she'd never burned him when it came to "the ends." And even though she was starting to hate the ground he walked on, she still wasn't about to start spending his money without his say. That would have sent up a red flag. Then what excuse would she have given him? Instead, she turned an extra trick when she could, just to cover the cost of the additional room she'd added to their tab.

"God help me!" Halleigh cried out once again, gripping her stomach in agony. That's when the irony of it all hit. She was exactly where God probably wanted her to be in order for Him to get her to call out to Him, on her knees.

In all of the mess she had been in since the night of the rape, she had not once gone to God and asked Him for help. She went to Malek, Mimi, Manolo. And, regretfully, she'd gone to Scratch. But not once did she just go to the one who was in charge of everything and ask Him to show her the right way to go about life.

As Halleigh began to call out to God with her last breath, it seemed, she only hoped it wasn't too late. But figuring that she didn't have anything to lose since she had given up everything, right down to her soul, she began to pray. Hopefully she could convince God to talk to Satan and order him to give her back her soul.

Halleigh folded her hands and leaned over the bed. Every movement ached her healing bones. For all of those days in that hotel room with the television on, she remembered hearing some tele-vangelist speak about the power of prayer, but had never partaken in it herself. She was willing to try anything now to take the pain away, though. Since all else failed, perhaps prayer wouldn't.

The pressure on her knees was too much to take. She fell down on her side and began to cry. She figured that she didn't have to be on her knees in order for God to hear her, so she let the tears come as she put her hands up to her face.

God, please help me. I know that you shouldn't, and I am probably not worth saving, but haven't I suffered enough? You blessed my life when You brought Malek into it. Before him, I didn't know love. I would have never imagined knowing another person better than I know myself. You already know how my mother gets down, so I don't have to go into that whole situation, and I'm not looking for a pity party, because I know that I did this to myself. Life just hurts so bad, God. It hurts. Malek doesn't want me anymore. He won't even see me. He was my everything, God, my reason for breathing. What did I do to deserve losing him?

I don't know if I can handle life without him. That's why I'm lying here on this floor with a drug-infested body. I poisoned myself trying to soothe my heart, shooting dope, free-basing. I did whatever I had to do to forget about Malek and the life I'm living. I'm killing myself slowly, but I know that I'm wrong. But I can't fix it by myself. It hurts so bad. My body hurts all day. It feels like I can't breathe.

I'm begging You, God, to take this burden away from me. I can't handle it. I'm not strong enough. I know I've never come to You before. I don't go to church every Sunday like some of the other people who call on You might, but I do believe that You can save me. If I am Your child,

*why does my life hurt so badly? Why me? Please save me
from this because I don't think I'm strong enough to do
this without Your support. I don't want to do this to myself anymore. I'm dying.*

Halleigh became too weak to even think. Her
prayer stopped short as her eyes became too heavy
for her to keep them open. Her arms fell to her
sides as she just lay there.

Tasha entered the hotel room and saw Halleigh
sprawled out on the floor near the bed. "Oh God!"
She dropped her purse and ran over to Halleigh.
"God, please don't let her be dead. Please don't let
her be dead."

Tasha made it over to Halleigh, got on her
knees, and grabbed her wrist to check for a pulse.
She then placed her ear against Halleigh's nose,
trying to see if she could feel any life coming out
of her, something she'd seen on television before.

Halleigh coughed.

"Oh Jesus!" Tasha said with a sigh of relief. "Hal,
why are you laying out on the floor like this?"
Tasha sat beside her on the floor and rubbed her
hair softly.

Halleigh opened her eyes and replied, "No,
Tasha, don't touch me. It hurts." She was too fa-
tigued to even cry. Tears just drained from her
eyes and rolled down the side of her face. "It just
hurts so bad," she whispered.

"I know, I know, Hal. I'm so sorry for this. I
know that this ain't for you. This isn't for anybody.
You don't deserve this. I don't deserve this. I'm
going to get us out of here. Just let me come up
with a plan. I just need to think of a way to get us

away from Manolo safely. Just hang in there. Give me time. I swear, I'm going to find a way out."

"I thought you said there is no way out," Halleigh replied, feeding Tasha's own words back to her.

"I'll find a way, Halleigh. I'll find a way," Tasha muttered as she tried to think of a possible escape plan for them. She pulled a cover and two pillows off the bed and lay right beside Halleigh. She snuggled close to her, wrapped her arms around her, and let the tears fall without shame.

It had been so long since she had cried. She'd trained herself not to be emotional from the day she turned her first trick. She didn't want anyone to think she was weak or that she could be easily manipulated, so she told herself that crying was a sure way to lose control over her own life. Now she felt weak, trapped underneath Manolo's selfish reign, and all she really felt like doing was crying.

As Tasha lay next to Halleigh, she cried for all of the times that she'd let strange men have her body. For all of the souls of the girls she'd helped Manolo lure in. For her parents, whom she knew she'd hurt when she started tricking. And for Loita. When Loita died, she didn't even cry then, so she was crying for her now too.

She released her entire life's heartache while she lay next to Halleigh, and she felt a closeness with her now more than ever before. Tasha knew that it was time for her to get strong—on her own. She didn't want to feel powerful by preying on the weakness of others, but she wanted to empower both herself and Halleigh so that they could live the life that they deserved.

God surely must have taken these two women to the bottom this day, to a point where they both realized that they had nowhere to go to and no one to go to but Him. It seemed that prayer was moving in Tasha's heart that day as well, because she asked God for the strength she needed to get them out of their current situation, and to give her a better direction in life.

Chapter Twenty

Two weeks passed by, and each day God answered Halleigh's prayers by gradually taking the pain away. Halleigh was no longer in unbearable pain, but she was still very weak. She honestly didn't know what it was that was causing her pain to be less severe; whether it was prayer, God, or if her body was just getting better on its own now that she wasn't feeding it heroin anymore.

Also, to help ease her pain, Tasha had tricked with a doctor who gave her a prescription of methadone for Halleigh that made her body think it was getting a hit, but it really wasn't.

Now that she was getting better, Halleigh was tired of being locked up in the hotel room. Before, she could barely move, so staying in that hotel room wasn't an issue. But now she felt cooped up and nauseated all the time. She figured that her body was still trying to adjust.

She had polluted her body with drugs, and now that she wasn't on them anymore, she felt weird, but she was grateful to be alive. She realized what a stupid mistake she'd made. She didn't want to be addicted to drugs. For her entire life, she had tried to differentiate herself from her mother. She wanted to show people that she wouldn't follow in her mother's footsteps, but indeed, she had fallen victim to the trials and tribulations of the streets.

Halleigh knew that she was very lucky to have her life. She had been spared. For what reason? She didn't know, but she promised herself that she would never take her life for granted again. Not for Malek, not for anyone.

After Tasha told Halleigh how Malek had refused to help her, Halleigh had tried to wrap her mind around the fact that he didn't care anymore. That simply broke her heart. But she'd found a new friendship with Tasha, who really had become like a sister to her. Before, it was Mimi and Halleigh who had been the closest, but Mimi had been on a paper chase, putting the almighty dollar before everyone and everything. Tasha, too, was on the paper chase, but not because she was obsessed with money like Mimi was. She was doing it for the sake of Halleigh. Tasha and Halleigh talked together, laughed together, cried together, and dreamed big together. They also promised each other that they would always keep in contact, no matter where their lives took them.

Tasha promised Halleigh that she would still try to help her see Malek again, if that's what she really wanted, even if it was just for closure. But first things first, Tasha had to get her and Halleigh out of Manolo's clutch.

Halleigh knew that Tasha was trying to get her out of the game, but what she didn't know was that Tasha herself wanted out of the life as well.

"How do you feel?" Tasha asked Halleigh, who was sitting on the bed playing a game of solitaire with a deck of cards Tasha had bought her from the corner store, so she could focus her mind on something. Tasha had just finished up a long night of work.

"Better." Halleigh continued her game, not looking up at Tasha. Not only was Halleigh ashamed that Tasha was out turning tricks because of her, but she was embarrassed by her own behavior.

Tasha noticed her disposition. "Ain't no need to feel no type of way around me. You're my sister. I did what I had to do to make sure you were okay, so don't look down on yourself. You know these past few weeks we've sort of switched places. Turning tricks will tear you down mentally and physically. I understand how it broke you, Hal, but you have to promise me that you are going to take care of yourself. You've got to stay strong from here on out. No more drugs. Having to cover for you and turn tricks to make sure that Manolo's money was consistent made me realize that this lifestyle ain't for me either. I realize now that it was never for you. We'll get away from Manolo. I don't know how yet, but we will. Just give me some time to figure it out, okay?"

Halleigh nodded her head. "Okay," she stated, still not looking up.

"Now, you ready to get out of this hotel to get some fresh air? I know you have to be starving."

Halleigh didn't think that she would be able to hold down any food. The way her stomach felt, the food would probably make her sick. She was also still having a hard time controlling her bowels. She stood up and looked at herself in the mirror, and what she saw disgusted her. She'd lost about twenty-five pounds, and her skin was sickly-looking. She barely recognized the person staring back at her.

"Yeah, from the looks of it, I need to eat," she said, figuring she'd at least give it a try. If nothing else, she would at least enjoy some fresh air. She felt like a prisoner in solitary confinement, although she was the one who'd created her own prison.

"Then let me go get cleaned up real quick," Tasha told her, "and then we'll head out." Tasha headed over to the bathroom.

"Cool," Halleigh replied.

At that exact moment, Mimi came banging on Tasha's door, stopping Tasha right in her tracks at the doorway. "Tasha, open up!" Mimi yelled. "I know you in here."

Halleigh looked at Tasha nervously.

Tasha whispered, "Don't worry about it. I didn't tell her anything about what's been going on. She just thinks you've been sick."

Halleigh breathed a sigh of relief. She didn't want her business to be out there like that, and was grateful that Tasha hadn't spread the news. Halleigh liked Mimi, but she knew Mimi's relationship with Benjamin Franklin took precedence over any friendship.

Tasha nodded at Halleigh to go ahead and open the door for Mimi, which she obliged.

When the door opened, Mimi practically knocked Halleigh down when she saw her. "Bitch, where the hell have you been?" she asked as she hugged her tightly.

"Ow, Mimi!" Halleigh whined, grimacing slightly from Mimi's tight grasp.

"Take it easy, Mimi," Tasha said. "She's still a little under the weather."

"Um, no offense," Mimi said, looking Halleigh up and down, "but you do look bad." She then walked over to Tasha to talk about the business at hand: the fresh gossip that had her anxious to spill.

"Girl! Keesha lying ass been spreading all types of rumors around this bitch about where Halleigh been. First, she was talking about Halleigh was pregnant, and I was like uh-uh, 'cause I knew you wouldn't have kept that from me." Mimi turned to Halleigh. "Then she started talking about how Halleigh had caught something from one of her johns and gave it to Manolo. She said that he had her taken care of. I knew that shit was a lie too, though."

Halleigh and Tasha were cracking up at Mimi, who couldn't stop talking. She was going on and on about how much drama Halleigh had missed and how much she hated Keesha.

"Tasha, will you please let me beat that bitch's ass for lying on my girl?" Mimi said, getting even more amped at the thought of fighting Keesha.

"No, let it go, Mi," Tasha told her. "She ain't worth it. Anyway, I'm about to freshen up. Hal and I are about to go grab something to eat."

Tasha continued into the bathroom, but before she closed the door, Mimi mocked, "Hal and I are about to go grab something to eat," and threw Tasha a nasty look.

"You got a problem?" Tasha said, stepping to her.

"No, just that you are all of a sudden treating me like some stepchild, like I ain't a part of y'all's little clique." She turned back to Halleigh and said, "I asked her a thousand times about what was going on with you, and she wouldn't tell me anything except that you were sick. Well, what kind of sick?"

"That's 'cause you didn't need to know nothing, bitch," Tasha said playfully. "And don't get jealous, ho. You can come eat with us too if you want," Tasha said, closing the bathroom door.

"You paying?" Mimi asked through the door, her hands on her hips.

"Yeah, it's on me." Tasha shook her head from side to side at Mimi's cheap self.

A few minutes later, Tasha came out of the bathroom and grabbed her purse. "Y'all ready to eat or what? Come on, let's go celebrate." Tasha winked at Halleigh.

"What are we celebrating?" Mimi asked, feeling like she was on the outside of an inside joke.

"We are celebrating that our Halleigh's health is coming back and that everything is good now." She turned to Halleigh. "So where you want to eat, guest of honor?"

"It ain't got to be nothing all big. Let's just go to

Atlas Coney Island," she replied. "Hopefully I can get a hot dog down at least."

Tasha smiled, and the girls headed out of the room, Mimi leading the way and Halleigh behind her.

"I'm proud of you," Tasha whispered to Halleigh as she put her arm around her shoulders and they headed out. Tasha was also proud of herself for pulling Halleigh out of the gutter. Now all she had to do was make sure that they both kept their heads above water until they found rescue.

Chapter Twenty-one

Jamaica Joe, Tariq, and Malek loaded up the black Navigator with several duffle bags containing twenty kilos of pure cocaine. Joe had a buyer in Detroit who wanted to get hit off. Joe usually never made transactions face to face with his buyers, but because of the big order, he decided to make the trip himself. He couldn't afford to take any risk with some other cat fucking up his money.

Sweets' little caper had set Joe back, and he was trying to get his paper back up to par. He needed this flip desperately, and wasn't going to trust anyone else with that amount of money. He would make $350,000 on the transaction, and didn't want any funny business with one of his mules, or some nigga getting caught slippin' and getting robbed. He asked Malek and Tariq to come along for added security, and made sure they were prepared before they hit the road.

Joe loaded the last bag into the trunk. "Yo, you strapped up?" he asked Malek.

"You know it," Malek said in a low tone as he patted his waist.

"You?" Joe asked Tariq as he looked over in his direction.

"Yep!" Tariq lifted his shirt and displayed his twin 9 millimeter pistols.

They all jumped into the truck and took off. Malek drove, and Tariq sat up front in the passenger's seat, while Joe sat in the back and lit up a blunt.

'Bout time this nigga chauffeured my ass around for a change, Tariq thought as he pulled out his Sidekick. *Now, this shit is more like it.* He leaned back and got comfortable, reclining his seat a little. He looked over at Malek. *Although it's too little, too late, as far as I'm concerned. But still, I'ma milk this shit for all it's worth.*

"Yo, let's stop at Atlas restaurant and grab something to eat before we hit the road. I'm hungry as hell," Joe said as he leaned back in his chair and inhaled the weed smoke into his lungs.

They all bobbed their heads in unison to Jay-Z's *Reasonable Doubt,* which was pumping lightly out of the subwoofers in the trunk, as they headed toward the restaurant.

Malek kept noticing how Tariq was continuously typing on his Sidekick. He was wondering if Joe had peeped it, but then his question was answered when he heard Joe say, "Nigga, you always on that mu'fucka, sweet-talking them hoes."

Tariq hurriedly put his Sidekick away. "Man, ain't nobody sweet-talking nobody."

"Yeah right, nigga. You probably over there caking it, paying car notes and all," Malek added.

"Yeah right," Tariq responded, noticeably irritated. *I'ma be caking, all right, nigga. Just wait and see.*

"Please don't kill me, Sweets! Please. I got three kids at home. I'm sorry," the man pleaded while on his knees. Sweets had found out that he was skimming off of the top and stepping on the dope to make more money. The man had been stealing from Sweets for years and had finally gotten caught.

"You stupid mu'fucka, why would you steal from me, huh?" Sweets slapped dude upside the head, like he was some young schoolboy getting popped by his mama for not cleaning up his room. "Don't I treat you good? When yo' bitch-ass ex-wife took yo' house, who helped you get on yo' feet? I gave you a job, and this is how you repay me. You stepping on my dope, having fiends run to the North Side because my product is weak. That's bad business, my nigga! You fuckin' with my money. Now you gotta pay. It ain't a game, fam!" Sweets grabbed his long machete from behind his desk.

The grown man began to cry like a little child, begging and pleading for his life. The sight of the long machete made his limbs shake uncontrollably. He knew something bad was about to happen to him, and he instantly began to regret skimming money from Sweets.

"Pick his ass up and turn him around!" Sweets ordered two of his soldiers, who stood in the room with him.

Lynch and another one of Sweets' henchmen grabbed the man and turned him around to face the wall.

"Don't move, mu'fucka!" Sweets said as he raised his machete.

The man knew that Sweets was about to cut his ass up. He'd heard stories about how crazy Sweets was. His body tensed up as he waited for his life to end. He kept visualizing Sweets chopping off his head with that long machete.

"Please, Sweets, don't kill me." The man decided to plead one last time as he faced the wall, not knowing how he was about to die. He began to sweat profusely. All he could do was beg for his life. "Please, Sweets, please, man. I'll never steal another thing in my life."

The sound of plastic being ripped filled the air as Sweets stood behind the man. He didn't know what it was, but he would soon find out. All of a sudden, the man heard the sound of the machete slicing through the air. The man closed his eyes, preparing himself to be decapitated. But when he didn't feel a knife pierce his skin, he slowly opened his eyes and saw that Sweets had other plans in mind. Sweets had cut the man's belt off, causing his pants to fall to his ankles. The man finally got the picture. He begged Sweets to stop, but the pleas fell on deaf ears. The ripping sound that he'd heard was Sweets opening a condom wrapper.

"You take my money, I take your manhood. If you

move, I'm going to slice yo' mu'fuckin' throat."
Sweets pulled down the man's boxers and grabbed
himself.

Lynch turned his back to avoid witnessing the
scene. Sweets often degraded men who stole from
him in that sort of way. *I hate when he do this shit.
This is some twisted gay shit, fam.* Lynch walked out
of the room.

Sweets bent the man over and rested his dick on
the man's back. "If you move, I'ma slice yo' mu'-
fuckin' throat. You got that?" Sweets took the knife
and slightly punctured the man's neck. Blood
trickled from the crying man's flesh as Sweets prepared to force himself in.

Just before Sweets could enter, his phone began
to vibrate on his hip. He smacked his lips, irritated
with the interruption, and pulled the phone off
his hip. He had a new text message that read: ATLAS
IN TEN MINUTES—20 BRICKS IN DA TRUNK.

"Oh shit!" Sweets said out loud gleefully. A huge
smile covered his face as he immediately pulled up
his pants and pushed the man forcefully to the
ground. "You got lucky this time, mu'fucka. You
steal from me again, though, and I guarantee you
won't get off so easy the next time," Sweets said as
he grabbed his gun and jacket. He had someone
to meet.

"Thank you, Sweets, thank you," the man said
while tears ran down his eyes. He'd just escaped an
ass-thrashing, literally. "I promise it will never happen again. God bless you, Sweets. God bless you,"
the man repeated as he pulled up his pants.

"Nigga, get the fuck out of here with all that crying," Sweets said. He thought to himself, *Damn! And I was gon' tear that ass up. But hell, money over dick.* "Load up! Joe at Atlas. Let's get 'em!" Sweets yelled loud enough for his soldiers to hear him in the next room.

Lynch rushed into the room, not believing what he'd just heard. He was itching to get at Joe, to avenge the death of his little brother.

"His man just hit me up saying that they're going to be at Atlas in ten minutes. Let's roll." Sweets zipped up his pants.

"What you going to do with ol' dude?" Lynch said, throwing his head in the thief's direction.

Sweets looked at the man and contemplated what to do with him. He knew he couldn't just let him get out of there scot-free, with no conse-quences whatsoever. That would be bad for busi-ness. Then every mu'fucka might think they could get away with stealing from Sweets. He finally said, "Give 'im a limp." Sweets headed out the door.

"No doubt." Lynch pulled out his gun, pointed it at the man's leg, and left two bullets in it. *Bang! Bang!* "Hope you wasn't an NBA prospect too." Lynch chuckled.

The man screamed in agony while Sweets and the Shottah Boyz rushed over to Atlas restaurant to give Joe's crew a rude awakening.

Chapter Twenty-two

Halleigh entered the twenty-four-hour restaurant along with Tasha and Mimi. The Manolo Mamis were in the building, and all eyes were on them as they strolled in. Halleigh was still beautiful, although her recent struggles showed in her face and loss of weight. She looked tired and worn out, but she was proud of herself for being brave enough to fight her drug addiction. Although she hated what Tasha did to her at the time, handcuffing her to the bed and not allowing her to leave the room, she loved her for it now and understood exactly why she had done it. Had she not, as far as Halleigh was concerned, she could be lying dead in an alley somewhere.

Tasha had opened Halleigh's eyes and made her realize that she was following in her mother's footsteps. She would have eventually found herself at the point of no return, but thanks to Tasha's support, she didn't finish the path she was heading down. It was only the beginning of Halleigh's recovery, but it was a start.

Tasha was only few years older than Halleigh, but she showed her motherly love at the time Halleigh needed it the most. Halleigh looked at Tasha and smiled, and Tasha returned the smile, proud of the way Halleigh shook the monkey off her back.

Among the patrons who looked their way when the girls entered the restaurant was Malek. His heart sank into his stomach when he saw Halleigh. She wasn't the same Halleigh he'd seen just a few months ago. She looked as though she'd taken an ass-whippin' from the streets.

What the fuck happened? Malek looked her up and down. But then he heard the sound of Tasha's words echoing through his head. *"She needs you,"* he remembered her telling him, and from the looks of things, he knew that it was true.

Malek couldn't take his eyes off of her, and his heart beat so loudly in his chest that he was sure Jamaica Joe and Tariq could hear it. Malek's heart dropped at the sight of Halleigh. He noticed that she had lost weight, and her eyes looked baggy. He knew something wasn't right with her, and that's probably what Tasha had been trying to warn him about. His pride wanted him not to stare, but his heart made his eyes stick on her.

No matter what Halleigh and Malek had gone through, he still loved her. Halleigh might have been able to shake drugs, but Malek couldn't seem to shake her.

For the last couple of months, Malek, trying to keep Halleigh off his mind, was just getting with chicks for the hell of it. But whenever he was inside one of them, he couldn't help but picture Halleigh's face.

"Who the fuck is Halleigh?" one of the girls spat to him as she sat butt naked on top of him, riding the hell out of him.

She was putting her back into it when all of a sudden he had yelled, "Oh, Halleigh, baby, don't stop!"

Although Malek was never intimate with Halleigh, he had dreamed about it a million times. He had played that night in his head after his high school championship game, when she had promised him her virginity, imagining how it would be—how it would feel to be inside of her, to be the first man ever inside of her. It would have been such a privilege. He knew he was going to wife her. But then everything took a turn for the worse when he dropped her off at her house after the game so she could freshen up for him. It was then that two men savagely raped her and stole her innocence. To this day, Malek wanted revenge on those two fools just as much as he wanted revenge on whoever took his parents out.

Halleigh finally looked in the direction where Malek and his crew were sitting, and when she saw him, her eyes almost popped out of her head. She stopped suddenly in her tracks.

"You all right, girl?" Tasha asked her. She followed Halleigh's eyes and saw Malek.

"Yeah," Halleigh lied. She wanted to believe that she was okay, but she wasn't.

"Come on," Tasha said, grabbing her arm. "Just let him be over there with his boys. If he wants to step to you, then so be it. Otherwise, let 'im be."

Halleigh didn't even realize that Malek was there with Jamaica Joe and Tariq. As a matter of fact, she almost forgot that she was there with Tasha and Mimi. When she and Malek had locked eyes, it felt as if the two of them were the only ones in the room.

"Yeah, you're right," Halleigh said as she took a couple more steps. She peeled her eyes off of Malek and let them fall on the two guys he was with. Once again she stopped dead in her tracks, but this time, she began to tremble.

"What is it, Hal?" Tasha asked, her eyes darting back and forth from Halleigh to Malek and his boys. "You okay?" Tasha could feel Halleigh's body trembling.

Halleigh just stood there with her mouth dropped open as she stared at Tariq. *That's him,* Halleigh thought. "That's him," she said out loud. Halleigh would never forget the faces of the men who raped her, and Tariq's face was one of them.

Her heart began to beat rapidly. She couldn't believe that Malek was sitting there with him—the man he was supposed to protect her from, the man he said he would kill if he ever found him. And now here the two of them were, about to break bread together.

Halleigh pulled her arm away from Tasha and hurried to the back of the restaurant, where the restrooms were located. She could barely breathe.

The sight of Malek with Tariq made her want to throw up.

She burst into the bathroom and rested both of her arms on the sink. She was tormented by horrific memories of the night her virginity was ripped away from her. The fact that Malek was sitting next to her rapist made her heart sink deeper in her chest. She couldn't believe it. "How could he?" she whispered as the tears in her eyes built up. "How could he?"

Chapter Twenty-three

"I'll be back," Malek said to Joe and Tariq as he made his way to the back of the restaurant. He knew Jamaica Joe probably had something to say about him going after Halleigh, but he couldn't hold off any longer. He had to talk to her.

He paced outside of the bathroom, waiting for Halleigh to come out.

"Yo, come on, man," Joe called out. "We got business."

Malek acted like he didn't hear him and just continued pacing until he heard the women's bathroom door open. He caught Halleigh on her way out. "Halleigh!" he whispered as he grabbed her arm.

"Get away from me, Malek," she said, trying to pull away.

"No, I need to talk to you. Just listen to me for a minute," Malek said while Halleigh struggled to get away from his grip, using up the little bit of energy left in her body.

Malek got tired of struggling with her and ended up pushing her into the men's bathroom and into one of the stalls. But she pulled away from him, not wanting anything to do with him. She was inconsolable.

"Don't touch me," she said weakly. His touch hurt her sensitive body, but she also didn't want his hands on her since he was associating with the person who'd raped her. Halleigh couldn't believe that Malek was with a man that had hurt her so bad. After she got raped, it sparked a chain of events that changed her life forever. In her mind, Malek was just as lowdown as the hoodlum he was sitting with.

"Are you okay?" Malek cupped her face in his hands and stared into her lost eyes. "What happened to you? Baby, I'm sorry. I should've come to you," Malek said as he got an up close and personal look at just how bad Halleigh appeared. She was "Whitney Houston skinny."

"Stop touching me," Halleigh said. "I can't believe this. How could you be with him? How could you?"

"What? Who? What are you talking about?"

Just then, the men's bathroom door opened. "Yo, Malek!" Tariq called out as he entered the bathroom.

Malek closed the stall door and replied, "What up?"

"It's time to go," Tariq said. "Joe trying to get on the road."

The sound of Tariq's voice sent chills up Halleigh's spine. The same way she could never forget his face, she could never forget his voice.

"All right, I'll be out in a minute," Malek said in an irritated tone. The only thing on his mind was Halleigh.

When Tariq left the restroom, Halleigh snatched away from Malek once again.

"Just let me go, Malek!"

"I will let you go, but on one condition . . ." Malek paused before continuing. "Leave with me, Hal."

Halleigh let out a sarcastic laugh.

"I'm serious. You're not looking too good. Let me take care of you. We can start over, just me and you."

"Let you take care of me?" Halleigh repeated. "Let you take care of me? You mean the same way you been taking care of me? Fuck you, Malek!"

"Fuck me? You the one who picked that other nigga over me, and you got the nerve to have an attitude with me?"

"It looks like you picked your niggas over me," she replied, her eyes flooded with tears. Malek's betrayal hurt more than anything she'd ever felt.

"What the fuck are you talking about?"

"Let me ask you one question, Malek. Since when did you start fucking with the nigga that raped me? Huh? He's what started all this. He raped me, and you're running around here with him like y'all best friends," Halleigh yelled, the warm tears gracing her cheeks.

Her words hit Malek like a ton of bricks.

"Y'all cut from the same cloth, Malek?" She began beating on Malek's chest. "You a rapist too? Huh? Is that what you were going to do to the girl in that room the night of that party before you saw that it was me?"

"Whoa, hold up," Malek said, putting up his hands. "You trying to say my boy Joe was one of the dudes that raped you?"

"I don't know his fuckin' name. The one you just told you'd be out in a minute," Halleigh said furiously. "What? Are you two on your way to rape somebody else?"

Malek tried to digest everything Halleigh was spitting at him. Finally, Halleigh mustered up every ounce of strength she had in an attempt to shove Malek out of her way, but Malek grabbed her.

"Get your hands off me," she said. "Don't touch me! Don't you ever touch me again," Halleigh screamed with so much rage that Malek released her. Then she squeezed past him and stormed out of the bathroom.

"Wait, Halleigh!" he yelled out, but Halleigh never looked back. Still in a daze, Malek exited the bathroom stall and began pacing again. "I can't believe this shit." He balled his fist and began punching the walls in the restroom as he tried to calm down.

Halleigh's words had hit him like a dagger, and he couldn't fathom someone hurting her again. He was determined to make things right for them. She was his soul mate, and he wasn't going to lose her again. The thought of Tariq raping Halleigh emerged in his mind, and he instantly became enraged. He pulled out his gun and cocked the hammer back. *I'ma murder that nigga.*

Just like Halleigh had accused him, he felt guilty, as if he were one of the men who'd raped her. All of this time he'd had no clue that Tariq was one of the men who'd hurt Halleigh on that horrible night, but now that he knew, he was going to make Tariq pay.

Chapter Twenty-four

Malek walked out of the restroom with rage in his eyes, his temple pulsating from the range of emotions he was experiencing. He watched as Halleigh, the woman he loved from the depths of his soul, rushed out of the restaurant with Tasha and Mimi.

He then focused his attention on Tariq, who was seated next to Jamaica Joe. His blood boiled as he closed his eyes and envisioned the hurtful expression that had covered Halleigh's face. Things had definitely shifted from what Malek thought they seemed. All along, he had been thinking that it was Halleigh who was, in fact, sleeping with the enemy by fucking with Manolo, when it was actually Malek himself that was cliqued up with one of the dudes that had raped her.

Just then, Malek became suspicious of everybody who was assigned under Tariq. Was it one of them who had gone to Halleigh's mom's apartment that night and participated in the assault? Malek's mind was twisted. He didn't know what his next move should be. Should he find out who the other cat was that helped Tariq and take them both out, or should he just kill Tariq's ass and ask questions later?

Malek looked out the window and saw Halleigh hop into the passenger's side of Tasha's car. He had to admit, he did love her. He felt like a traitor for associating with people who had harmed her. But now wasn't the time for him to stand there and beat himself up. He had a vendetta to take care of.

When Jamaica Joe saw Malek heading back their way, he stood and threw a fifty dollar bill on the table. He then walked over to Malek. "Everything's good?" Joe asked, noticing the distressed look on his face.

Malek nodded. He wasn't sure if he should tell Joe about the situation. He knew that Tariq was Joe's man way before he'd entered the picture, so he wasn't trying to create bad business by spitting venom on Joe's right-hand man. *I'ma handle that nigga myself when the time is right*, Malek assured himself and then turned to Joe and said, "Yeah, man, everything is good."

"Good, then let's get out of here. Time is money and—" Before Joe could finish his sentence, the sound of his car alarm going off caught his attention. "Fuck is going on?" he asked as he hurried outside.

Malek ran out behind him and exchanged cold stares with Tariq as he passed.

"'Sup, dude?" Tariq asked him aggressively, peep-ing out how Malek had just mean-mugged him like he had a problem with him or something.

Malek stopped in his tracks as Joe kept moving. Joe wasn't concerned about what was happening between his two soldiers. He was only concerned about his car, or better yet, the goods he had inside his car.

Malek stepped into Tariq's space. "What, mu'-fucka?" he said, blatantly showing him disrespect as he stared down at him. "You got a problem?"

Before the confrontation could escalate, gunshots rang out in the air.

"Oh shit! Joe!" Malek pushed past Tariq and ran outside, his pistol drawn.

Tariq ran out after him, and they both started busting, no questions asked, at Jamaica Joe's truck, his Viper car alarm blaring loudly as bullets whizzed through the air.

The back of Jamaica Joe's truck was open, and by the time they made their way over to the truck, blasting the entire way, Malek immediately peeped that the duffel bag full of bricks was missing. The gunfire was so hectic that everybody had to take cover. Joe, Tariq, and Malek were tucked behind a car in the parking lot, while Sweets, Manolo, and the Shottah Boyz ducked behind Joe's truck.

"Fuck! They got the joints," Joe stated in a frustrated tone. He pulled a full clip out of his pants pocket and loaded it into his gun. "I'm tired of playing around with this gay mu'fucka!"

Boom! Boom!

Bullets crashed the windows of the car they were crouched behind, sending glass flying everywhere.

Boom! Boom! Boom!

Malek shot back. He saw Manolo peek from behind Joe's truck and shot relentlessly at him.

Boom! Boom! Boom! Boom! Boom!

Jamaica Joe looked at Tariq, who was crouched low, hiding from the bullets, while Malek was a true soldier, standing his own against the hit squad. "Nigga, fuck you doing?" he yelled to Tariq. "Go get my bricks!" Joe reached over the car hood and fired a shot.

By now Joe's truck looked like Swiss cheese, but that was the last thing on his mind. He couldn't afford to take this loss. He had to get his dope back.

Tariq stood up and pulled out his gun. He shot in Sweets' direction, making sure not to hit any of his crew, firing shots indirectly.

Malek was a madman, taking out all of his anger on Sweets and his crew. What he really wanted to do was blast on Tariq's ass, but that opportunity would have to present itself at a later date. Right now his target was Manolo. He'd hurt Halleigh too. And from this point on, Malek was getting ready to get at any nigga who had even looked at her wrong in the past.

His gun spat, *Boom! Boom! Boom!*

All of a sudden, Tariq stepped into Malek's line of view. Malek's gun was already aimed to hit him. All he had to do was pull the trigger. *This nigga raped my girl,* he thought as his finger twitched violently. *This nigga took what should've been mine.*

Malek had never killed a man, but he was tempted to let Tariq have his whole clip. He froze and stared at Tariq, his gun pointed at his back. Tariq had no idea that Malek was behind him with deadly intentions.

Jamaica Joe heard the sirens of the approaching police cars. They sounded as if they were right around the corner. He peered from behind the car, and his eyes bucked when he saw Malek aiming his pistol at the back of Tariq's head. *Fuck is he doing?* Joe thought.

Malek closed his eyes and pulled the trigger.

CLICK! The sound of the empty clip rang out, but Tariq didn't hear it.

Sweets ran and jumped back into his truck when he heard the police sirens, and was pulling wildly out of the parking lot as Tariq feigned to bust wildly at him.

Tears filled Malek's eyes. He regretted wasting his bullets on Sweets. *CLICK! CLICK!* He continued to squeeze the trigger anyway, even though he knew he had no ammunition.

Jamaica Joe ran up and put his hand on Malek's shoulder. "Whoa," he stated in Malek's ear as he took the gun from his hand. He didn't ask any questions, but he definitely wanted to know what was going on between Tariq and Malek. "Jacob!" he shouted, signaling to Tariq that the police were on their way.

Since their truck was all shot up, tires and all, Tariq busted out a window to another car in the restaurant parking lot. He quickly hot-wired the car and pulled off with Jamaica Joe in the front seat and Malek in the back.

Riding shotgun as Tariq maneuvered away from the shootout scene, Jamaica Joe turned around and eyed Malek suspiciously. "You a'ight, partna?"

Malek leaned across the back seat and nodded his head, murderous thoughts racing through his mind as he sat behind Tariq. "Don't like to leave business unfinished, that's all."

"Oh, we gon' finish that shit," Tariq stated, referring to the beef with the South Side. He tossed his pistol in the back seat and threw his head back in relief. He took a deep breath, knowing he had just sparked some deep shit. "This shit ain't over," he added, pretending he was ready to retaliate.

"No doubt," Malek responded, referring to his unresolved beef with Tariq. Malek's blood was boiling. He couldn't control himself anymore. He slowly picked up Tariq's banger and put it in his lap.

Tupac's song, "Hail Mary," was in the CD player, and Malek asked Tariq to turn it up a notch, but it wasn't because he wanted to hear the song. Once the music was up loud enough to conceal the sound, Malek cocked the pistol and pointed it to the back of Tariq's dome.

THE END
(of *FLINT* book 2)
. . . but the saga continues in *FLINT* book 3.

Turn the page for a sneak peek at
Teasure Hernandez's
Flint Book #3
Coming soon . . .

Chapter One

Halleigh looked in the mirror and saw a person who bore no resemblance to the young woman she used to be. It seemed like just yesterday she was an excelling senior in high school dating the most popular boy at school, who just happened to be the biggest up and coming basketball star since LeBron James. The two of them shared champagne dreams of him signing a lucrative NBA contract and then moving the two of them as far away from the city of Flint as possible. But now, more than a year later, she was a high school dropout, trickin' with johns for a living.

"What happened to me?" It was the question Halleigh asked herself as she recalled what once was. Before her recent days of whorin' and druggin', her life had been all planned out, and not one of her plans consisted of being pimped out to the highest bidder. She was supposed to marry

Malek—her rising superstar athlete, her savior—
and live happily ever after. She had wanted it all:
everything that being on the arm of an NBA star
offered. She had been ready to accept her position
as Malek's wifey.

Unfortunately, Halleigh's real life didn't live up
to her fairy tale fantasy. Her life had gone from
Heaven to Hell in the blink of an eye, and she'd had
enough. Halleigh watched the tears flow down her
face as she stood in front of the mirror. They weren't
tears of force that came from heaving and overreact-
ing. They were true tears of a broken, hopeless spirit,
and they stained her face as she looked down at the
gun in her hand.

The day Halleigh copped the gun, she had actually intended to ask her get-high buddy, Scratch, to
cop her some heroin instead. But then, on her way to
meet Scratch at their spot in the alley—where they
had initially met when he tried to rob her with a
stick concealed to look like a gun—she noticed how
people were looking at her now. Having been nothing short of a dime-piece, Halleigh was used to turning heads. She was used to the gawking of men and
the envious glares of women. But this time, the attention was different. They were stares of disgust
and pity.

As Halleigh walked by a used appliance store, she
caught a glimpse of her reflection in the window.
She stopped in her tracks and gasped at the frail
sight before her. Slowly, her hands began to roam
her face, just to confirm that the reflection was actually hers. Were those really her eyes she was looking
into? Once upon a time those eyes had been full of

life and energy, no matter how much negativity they had witnessed.

Halleigh allowed her hands to roam down her body. Wearing tight-fitting jeans with knee-high stiletto boots and a sequined top, she thought she looked just fine, but underneath her hands she could feel almost every bone in her body. Taking a long, hard look at herself, Halleigh, too, was disgusted by what she saw.

The store owner interrupted her when he came out of the store and asked if he could help her with anything. Without saying a word, she walked off crying. As far as Halleigh was concerned, what she had just seen wasn't her, but a disintegrating corpse of her former self. She was as good as dead. She felt like death. That was the moment she decided she was better off dead than living the way she had been.

When she asked Scratch to help her cop a gun, he wasn't for it at first. He was trying to get high with Halleigh's money, not waste it on a cold piece of metal. But after realizing that he could cop a gun and still have money left for a hit, he obliged her plea. She hadn't told him what she intended to do with the weapon. Now, Halleigh stood with the gun to her temple. The cold steel was pressed against her clammy skin, and her body reacted by breaking into a cold, nervous sweat.

Moments from her life flashed before her eyes— all the heartache and tragedy she'd experienced— and she had a drastic decision to make. To live or to die? To fight or to retreat? To win or to lose? She was tired of struggling to survive in a city that had no love for her. She was choosing death, and there was no turning back. Halleigh put her finger just above the trigger . . .

"Hal, what are you doing in there? Open the door!" Mimi's voice came from the other side of the bathroom door, where Halleigh had been locked in for the past half-hour.

Halleigh didn't respond.

"Halleigh?" Mimi called again. "Open the door. Why you locking doors around this mu'fucka? You know Manolo will have a fit."

Halleigh's arm shook uncontrollably as Mimi continued knocking. "Just pull the trigger," Halleigh whispered to herself. "All of the pain will go away. Just end it." A small cry escaped her lips and she lowered the gun.

"Halleigh? Are you all right? You crying? Open the door," Mimi said, her tone now filled with concern. When Halleigh failed to respond, Mimi sensed that something was terribly wrong.

"Tasha!" she turned around and yelled. "There's something wrong with Halleigh!"

Tasha's head appeared from behind her bedroom door. She wore only a bra and panties. "What do you mean something's wrong with her?" she asked.

"I mean she's in this mu'fucka with the door locked and she's crying." Mimi then began to whisper. "I don't want the bitch to do nothing crazy. You know she just been through all that shit with Malek."

"Fuck you whispering for, like she can't hear you?" Tasha asked as she walked up to the door and put her ear against it. She, too, could hear Halleigh whimpering.

"Hal, open up the door so we can talk," Tasha

urged, now somewhat concerned herself. She picked up where Mimi left off knocking on the door. "Halleigh, listen. Just open up the door," Tasha pleaded then turned around and stared at Mimi, her eyes wide with fright.

"I told you," Mimi said knowingly. After all the drama and heartache that Halleigh had experienced, Mimi wasn't surprised that she was flipping out.

Halleigh could hear them calling for her, but ignored it. She knew what she had to do, and she wasn't going to let anything distract her from doing it. She lifted the gun to her head again and cocked the semi-automatic.

Click, click.

"Was that a gun?" Mimi asked, but before Tasha could reply, they heard a loud sound coming from the bathroom.

Bam! Bam! Bam!

Tasha pounded her open hand frantically against the door. "Halleigh, open the damn door!" Tasha screamed desperately.

"Oh my God! She killed herself! She shot herself," Mimi shouted in a panic. "Tasha, do something!"

Tasha felt helpless. As the madam of the house, Tasha was supposed to keep all of the Manolo Mamis in line. This was why Manolo had appointed her to the job. But as a woman, Tasha also felt like she was supposed to protect them. She hated the fact that she might not have been able to protect one of the girls from her own self.

Tasha mustered up all her strength and threw her body against the bathroom door. When she finally broke it off its hinges, she raced into the bathroom to find Halleigh laid out on the floor.

The sound of the gunshot had been deafening as it ricocheted off the bathroom walls. The force had been so great that it knocked Halleigh off of her feet and onto the floor, where she lay, uninjured.

"Fuck is you doing?" Tasha screamed as she rushed over to Halleigh's side. Her shoulder throbbed from the impact of breaking into the bathroom door, but she disregarded the pain as she picked the gun up from the floor and handed it over her shoulder to Mimi.

"Hey, watch how you handling that thing," Mimi said, carefully taking it from Tasha's hand.

Tasha focused her attention on Halleigh, who was shaking like a leaf before her. Her cries built up in her throat as she struggled to contain her emotions. "Shhh, come here," Tasha comforted her. "It's okay, Hal. Everything is gon' be all right. I've told you that everything is going to be all right. You just gotta hold on, ma," she assured as she put her arms around her friend and rocked her slowly.

Mimi appeared back at the doorway after burying the gun in a drawer full of lingerie. She looked down at a visibly shaken Halleigh. "Is she all right?" she asked Tasha.

"Yeah, she's okay. She's gon' be fine," Tasha replied, still holding Halleigh tightly.

Mimi had never been one to get emotional. The only thing that made her cry was missing out on money, so when Tasha looked up and noticed that Mimi's eyes were full of tears, she outstretched her other arm to invite Mimi into the embrace. Mimi quickly filled in the circle and hugged Halleigh as well.

"It's time for this to stop," Tasha stated, her voice cracking. "We can't do this to ourselves anymore. Manolo is the only person getting something out of all this. He's beaten Hal down to the point where she feels she needs to take her own life. This is bullshit. Nobody should have that much power over us. Nobody!" Tasha had to fight back her own tears. "You and me, Mimi, we're a different breed. We're strong. We can handle this life better than Halleigh. But look at her. . . . Look what this is doing to her."

Mimi nodded, but said no words as Tasha continued. "First it was the drugs, and now this." Tasha shook her head.

Halleigh was too distraught to reply. She had just attempted to take her own life—and she might have succeeded if not for the fact that her heroin-wasted muscles couldn't even hold the weight of the gun to aim properly. Otherwise, her two friends would be weeping over a dead and bleeding corpse. But that's what Halleigh felt like, anyway: dead, and bleeding on the inside.

"Ain't no way we leaving Manolo and living to tell about it," Mimi stated. "You already know how he is, Tasha. So you tell me how we're supposed to get out of this situation. And if we do, how we gon' survive? All we used to is selling pussy. So what's the difference whether we're selling it for ourselves or Manolo? Selling pussy is selling pussy."

Tasha knew that Mimi's words were true. They couldn't just walk away from Manolo. He was Daddy, and would kill them before he let them leave. And even if she did find a way to pull the girls out from under Manolo's clutches, what would be their means of survival? She was stuck between a rock and a hard place. But that didn't deter her from wanting to escape from Manolo's iron-fisted rule.

"What are we gon' do?" Mimi asked again.

"Let me think. Damn!" Tasha replied, aggravated that she didn't have the answers to Mimi's queries on the top of her head. "For right now, just shut up and help me get Halleigh up from the floor."

Mimi gave her a questioning look, still wanting answers.

"Look, all I know is that I'm gonna have us out of here by the end of the week," Tasha stated.

Halleigh looked at Tasha, and an emotion finally registered on her face. It was a look of surprise, laced with disbelief. "I promise, Hal," Tasha reaffirmed. She didn't know how she was going to pull it off, but she knew she had to at least try . . . for the sake of all of them.

Chapter Two

Tasha pulled down the visor to check her make-up in the mirror before she exited the car. As she walked into the Flint Police Department, a look of contempt crossed her face. She hated the police and everything associated with them, but desperate times called for desperate measures. Heads turned as the police officers admired her shapely legs, which stretched out beneath the red shirt-like dress she had ordered from a Fredrick's of Hollywood catalog. It fit just tight enough to reveal the outline of her round behind.

As Tasha walked by officers who were just standing around shooting the breeze or updating one another on police business, she noticed the lustful stares, and a smirk crossed her face. *Your pockets can't afford this pussy. Fuckin' pigs.* She turned her nose up as she walked over to the front desk.

"What can I do for you?" an officer asked. He

was looking at the *Daily Journal* and never even looked up to acknowledge her.

"I'm here to see Detective Troy Davis," she responded.

Tasha figured that her visit to Officer Troy was long overdue. After all, he was the cop who Manolo supposedly had in his pocket—and it was Tasha's pussy that had sealed the deal. Her trick with Officer Troy was what had brought Tasha out of years of retirement, so as far as Tasha was concerned, he owed her one.

"Have a seat. I'll see if I can track him down," the officer responded.

Tasha nodded and sat with her legs crossed seductively in front of her. She massaged her legs suggestively as she waited for Officer Troy to come into sight. She needed his help and knew that she would have to give a little to get a little. She knew that she looked good. She had her fuck-'em dress on, and she was sure that Detective Troy Davis would take the bait.

"Miss Tasha," he called out.

She turned around to see Officer Troy standing there, looking his usual lame, bald-head self.

"To what do I owe this unexpected surprise?" Troy asked as he rubbed his hands together and approached her. He licked his lips as he looked her up and down.

This cornball-ass nigga, Tasha thought as she flicked her hair behind her shoulders. She did all she could to ignore the fact that Troy's bald-head was shaped funny, that he had had one doughnut too many, and worst of all, that he was part of Flint PD—a stinkin' cop. But she needed something, so she'd have to put on her game face and play her hand right. "Is there somewhere we can go to talk? You know, privately?" she asked, batting her eyes then allowing them to travel down to his crotch. It was only partially visible, due to the way his bulging gut hung over his belt.

"Yeah, let me show you to my office," he replied.

Tasha stood and followed him through the precinct. When he put his hand on the small of her back and massaged it gently, she knew that she had him right where she needed him to be. They went into a small, messy office and he pulled out a chair for her then took a seat behind his desk. He had closed his office door, leaving on the other side a few drooling fellow officers who wished they could be in his shoes.

"What can I do for you, Tasha? What is it that you want from me?" he asked as he leaned back in his chair and put his hands behind his head. He had intentions of getting her right where he wanted her, too. It was an open playing field right about now. It was anyone's game.

"Why does a girl have to want something?" she asked sweetly, giving him a genuine smile. He wasn't as naïve as she had assumed he was, and she knew that she would have to play her cards right in order to get him to help her out.

"Because you haven't said one word to me since our little rendezvous at Wild Thangs, and that was . . . what? Over a year ago?"

"Well, you know how it is in my line of work. A girl gets busy," Tasha reasoned.

"Oh, but now all of a sudden your busy schedule has permitted you to just show up here out of the blue looking for me?"

Tasha shrugged as if to say, "That's what it looks like."

"My luck ain't that good, sweetheart. So let's try this again. What can I do for you?"

Tasha knew it was time to change her strategy. She didn't want to insult Troy any further by making him think she was taking him for a fool. She was confident, however, that by the end of the day he'd been playing the fool anyway.

"Okay, I'm not gon' try to game you because I know you ain't falling for the bullshit anyway," she began.

"You damn right about that, shorty, so let's just be real," Troy stated.

Tasha smiled because she had Troy thinking that he was in control. Using reverse psychology, she was still gaming his ass, making it seem like he had the upper hand. She had to give herself a pat on the back because she was truly one of a kind. There wasn't a man alive who could outsmart her. Not even Manolo.

Tasha wasn't like the other girls when it came to Manolo. He hadn't had to trick or manipulate her into becoming a Manolo Mami. She knew exactly what she was getting into when she met South Side's most notorious pimp. Her entire goal was to become a kept woman, and if proving her loyalty to this man meant selling pussy for a couple of years, then so be it. Tasha's initial plan had always been to become the madam, the ruler over all of the other girls. It just so happened that Tasha's plan came to fruition a little sooner than she had expected.

Unfortunately it wasn't only Tasha's hard work and loyalty that placed her on the throne, but a horrible incident that she would never forget for as long as she lived. Being the strong-headed fighter that Tasha had always been, she didn't let the brutal assault by one of her johns keep her down. Instead, she used it to her advantage and convinced Manolo not to put her back on the streets. Instead, he allowed her to be the madam of the house—the kept woman—without having to turn one trick for the rest of her life if she didn't want to.

When he made the decision, Manolo had taken into consideration the true loyalty Tasha had shown him. And besides, the madam of the house definitely had to be somebody with Tasha's personality . . . someone who the girls knew they couldn't run over even with a Mack truck. So Manolo showed her favor and obliged her request, taking Tasha off the streets and giving her charge over the girls. But now Tasha needed a favor from someone else.

"Okay, I need a favor," Tasha told Troy.

"So the plot thickens," he replied sarcastically.

She raised her eyebrows and looked at him like he was crazy before she replied, "Are you gon' let me finish?"

"I'm sorry, sexy. Go ahead."

"I need you to raid Manolo's club," Tasha said bluntly.

"What do you mean, for show or something?" Troy asked with a puzzled look on in his face. Manolo had been allowing Troy a free supply of pussy from the Manolo Mamis in exchange for "overlooking certain things." So he couldn't imagine why else Tasha, whom he had known to clearly be on Manolo's team, would want him to raid Wild Thangs, Manolo's strip club.

"No, not for show," Tasha corrected him. "For real." She moved in closer to Troy as if she was about to tell him something top secret. "He's got ten bricks and a little over fifty thousand dollars in a wall safe in his office," she admitted. She bit her tongue and knew that it was because she was snitching. Under any other circumstance, she wouldn't even be caught in a police station, but she figured Manolo had this coming to him. She had watched him manipulate the minds of young girls for years.

Tasha knew she played a role in the manipulation too, which was why she felt a responsibility to help Halleigh, and now Mimi too, get their lives back on track. This was the reason she was abandoning her principles and snitching in order to bring Manolo down. She couldn't take back the heartache, pain, and even the death that some of the prostitutes had suffered, but she could at least save others from it. If ever there was a time she needed redemption in her life, it was now. She hoped that her efforts wouldn't be in vain.

Troy sat up in his seat and looked Tasha directly in the eyes. "This ain't news to me. I know what goes on in that club. The thing is, Manolo got me on payroll. Or have you forgot?" He winked at Tasha and rubbed her thigh. "So I'm already getting my cut," he stated frankly, giving her one hard smack on the leg and then turning his chair away to let her know that he was not interested.

As far as Troy was concerned, Tasha hadn't brought any better deal to the table than he was already getting. In addition to free pussy from the Manolo Mamis, Manolo threw him money on the side. A bird in the hand was worth two in the bush, he thought.

"Believe me, that little cash Manolo throwing you ain't got shit on what's sitting inside that safe. I figure we could split the take fifty-fifty. That's twenty-five stacks . . . not to mention the potential profit from the bricks. That's two years' salary for you," Tasha stated, hoping she could convince Troy to see things her way. Otherwise, she'd have to walk out of his office with the risk of him ratting her out to Manolo. She knew would that would result in.

"Why would you be telling me this? Manolo's pimpin' your pretty ass. No offense, but you Manolo's bitch. What do you have to gain?"

Tasha thought long and hard. She thought about how she first met Manolo. She was new in town and he had put her on to a hustle. That she couldn't deny. But that was before he was hard in the pimping game, when he was just about getting money by any means necessary, not really finessing his business skills in the pimping game. And she had been strong enough to deal with everything that came with the life. Some of the girls he had turned out in the later years, however, had been too weak to survive the game.

Halleigh's face popped into her mind. She knew

that Halleigh was one of the weakest, and that it was only a matter of time before she was found dead somewhere. The way Tasha saw it, she already had enough blood on her hands; there wasn't room for more.

"My freedom is what I have to gain," Tasha finally replied. She stood from her chair and walked over to lock Troy's office door. He watched her every move. She closed the blinds and walked behind his desk.

Troy turned his chair to face her, and she lifted one knee to open his legs wide. Her hands massaged the bulge that was growing in his groin.

"I'm chasing my freedom, Troy, and I'll do *anything* to get it," she whispered in his ear.

"Anything?" he whispered back, and the lust made his voice seem deeper.

"Any . . . thing," she replied.

He slipped a finger between her legs and smiled when he noticed that she wasn't wearing any panties. He had to admit, Tasha was a woman determined to get what she wanted.

Tasha's beauty had always enabled her to hustle men, and he was merely another victim on her long list of those conquered. Troy stood up and bent Tasha over his desk. Her voluptuous ass was calling for him, and he grinded against it as he undid his belt buckle.

Tasha played in her pussy, opening herself up for Troy and massaging her clitoris. She pulled a condom out of her bra and slid it to him. Troy was working with a good nine inches. He rubbed his bare thickness against her vaginal walls before slipping the condom on. He wanted to get just a touch of her rawness. After putting on the condom, Troy played with Tasha's womanhood with the tip of his penis.

Tasha was hot, and licked on her own nipples as she anticipated Troy entering her. He slid into her with ease and pumped her so hard that he caused her to crash against the desk. Items flew to the floor as she bucked against him and contracted her pussy on his shaft. He gripped her ass and opened and closed her cheeks as he rocked in and out of her. The sight of her slim waist, round behind, and the sound of her titties bouncing only excited him more. He began to moan in delight.

Tasha had to give it up to Troy; the nigga was fucking her right. If she had known that he was getting down like that, she might given his ass some pussy the last time they connected at the strip club. Instead, Troy had left the club with Tasha's pussy juice on his face only. But at the time, that had been enough to make her feel disgusted by what she'd had to do. Prior to that night, Tasha had taken on her role as madam and stopped participating in any sexual acts with anybody except for Manolo. So even though she was the one who ended up getting her rocks off with Troy's tongue action that night, a trick was a trick as far as she was concerned.

But now, she was actually enjoying herself. Tasha closed her eyes and bit her lip when Troy reached around and pinched her nipples. It turned her on, and before she knew it, she too was trying to silence her moans.

"Damn, this pussy so good," he whispered as his hips moved in circles, causing him to go even deeper inside of her. They were so loud that they had attracted a crowd outside of Troy's office.

Someone knocked loudly, but Troy ignored it. He pulled out of Tasha, turned her toward him and picked her up. He put his stiff dick inside her again. He pumped in and out of her while holding her in mid-air.

"Oh my God," she whispered in delight as he carried her around his office. He reached his office door and pressed her against it as he continued to sex her. He got so loud that she had to put her hand over his mouth.

"I'm about to nut," he exclaimed.

"Nut for me, baby," she whispered as she popped her pussy even harder, trying to get hers too. She felt the gush between her legs as she came, and a few seconds later, Troy gripped her ass tightly as he experienced the best orgasm of his life.

He put his hand around his length and pumped every single ounce of cum out of himself and into the tip of the condom as Tasha pulled her dress down and straightened it out.

"So, do we have a deal?" she asked.

"Yeah, baby, whatever you want," he replied breathlessly as he began to clean himself up with some napkins he removed from around a paper cup of coffee.

Tasha smiled. She was accustomed to getting her way. "Good. Do it tonight. Afterwards, we'll split everything up sixty-forty."

Troy frowned as he pulled up his slacks. "Sixty-forty? What happened to fifty-fifty?"

"This pussy ain't free," Tasha replied as she blew him a kiss. She opened the door to find a group of men standing there, eyeing her as if they were imagining what it would be like to be in Troy's shoes.

"Gentlemen," she greeted as she maneuvered between them and exited the building. She couldn't help the smile that spread across her face. She was about to gain her independence from Manolo.

Tasha also knew that afterwards, she, Halleigh, and Mimi would have to lay low. She decided that she would go back to her home town for a while until things cooled off. Thinking about the bricks she would soon have to unload, she knew just who could help her do it. She was looking forward to the future now. After tonight, Tasha hoped to be on the first flight back home to New York. She couldn't wait to share the good news with the Halleigh and Mimi as she made her way back to the house.

As Tasha drove, she thought momentarily about Manolo and what her betrayal would do to him. The more she thought about her relationship with him, the more she realized that Manolo had never done her wrong, not once since she had known him. He had always treated her like his main bitch, even before she was. As a matter of fact, it wasn't even his idea to put Tasha on the ho stroll in the first place— it was her own.

Although Tasha had witnessed Manolo beat a couple of the girls senseless, he had never laid a hand on her except to embrace her or make love to her. Come to think of it, Manolo was the first man in Tasha's life who hadn't hurt her, and this was how she was about to repay him?

All of a sudden, the sound of the tires rolling off of the paved highway lane and onto the berm startled Tasha out of her thoughts. "Oh, shit!" she said as she regained control of the car and positioned the vehicle back in its lane.

As Tasha continued driving, any fond thoughts of her and Manolo were suppressed by visions of everything she had witnessed him doing to the other girls, namely Halleigh and Mimi. She recalled how Manolo had beaten Mimi almost unconscious one night at Wild Thangs. She was so bruised up that she couldn't put in work for almost a month. Next she recalled the time Manolo beat Halleigh when she refused to give him head as he'd ordered.

Tasha realized that all the girls had taken one for the team by means of physical or mental abuse. Everyone but her. So, as she weighed her loyalty to Manolo against her sympathy for the girls, it was a no-brainer. Tasha stepped on the gas and said, "Fuck you, Manolo. I'm out for self now."

Chapter Three

Mimi was on stage working the pole as she looked out into the crowd. As always, Wild Thangs was packed and dollar bills scattered the stage during Mimi's show. A satisfying smile spread across her face as she looked at Manolo. He was sitting in his VIP booth with Tasha, Halleigh, and his young killers, The Shottah Boyz.

Manolo was poppin' bottles as if he was the king of the city, and Mimi could tell that he was feeling himself. According to the plan Tasha had shared with her earlier, his night was going downhill from there on out, and she reveled in the thought. She couldn't wait to see Manolo's downfall. After all the bad karma Manolo had put out into the world, he was finally about to get his.

Mimi reached high on the pole, gripping it with her hands. She wrapped her ankles around it, released her hands, and allowed her body to hang up-

side down. She then slowly slid down. Her little
trick caught Manolo's attention. He loved when she
did that move. She winked at him as she made her
way down to the bottom of the pole.

*Nigga, you better enjoy this night. It's gon' be your last
free night for a while,* she thought as she reached her
hands back up to grab the pole before her head slid
to the ground. She then proceeded to put her pussy
in a customer's face and grind. The man stuck out
his tongue and licked her slowly. He had full access
to her because of the crotchless camisole she was
wearing, and the crowd went crazy when they saw
the man feasting on her. Mimi wasn't embarrassed
or ashamed by her performance; she was all about
her paper. She had also made a name for herself as
one of the best dancers in Michigan, and wanted to
give her loyal fans a good finale. She knew that
tonight would be her last time stripping on anybody's pole. She was done with the entire ho business, and was ready to get money in a new way.

After her set, Mimi joined Manolo at his table.
He was drunk and feeling good when she sat down
beside him.

"Hey, Daddy," she greeted as she grabbed a drink
from his hand and took a sip.

"What up? You got my cut?" he asked, referring
to his percentage of her night's earnings.

His comment pissed Mimi off. He always tried to
pull his pimp card when he got around his niggas.
But she concealed her attitude as she reached in her
bra, pulled out her money and handed it over to
him. She figured that she would choose her battles
wisely. Besides, this one would be over soon. Tasha

had told her that she would split her sixty percent from the safe with her and Halleigh, so that they would at least have something to get them started once they were no longer working for Manolo. So, Mimi wasn't tripping over that money she had just given to Manolo.

She looked around at Halleigh and Tasha, who were sitting with one other Manolo Mami. Observing their smug expressions, Mimi could tell that they were feeling the same way she was—thick. They finally had the upper hand on Manolo, and he was so stuck on himself that he didn't even realize it.

Everybody was loose in the club, and Manolo was talking big as usual. They partied for hours, and at midnight, the club was popping off proper. Tasha checked her watch and knew what time it was. She scanned her surroundings discreetly. If everything was going according to plan, Troy would be there any minute.

Less than five minutes later, the club was flooded with uniformed police officers. They stormed into the club with their weapons drawn. A couple of screams erupted throughout, but few people were scared. Everyone put up their hands and watched nosily to see how the scenario was going to play out.

"Everybody on the ground! Now!" Troy screamed as he made his way to the VIP section with his fellow officers right behind him.

Manolo was enraged. *I'm paying this mu'fucka to turn his head to my business and he coming in here on some bullshit?* He stood to his feet.

"Fuck is going on, man? Thought we had a deal!" he spat as Troy approached.

Troy grabbed Manolo's arm and twisted him around, forcing him to lean over the table. The Shottah Boyz reached for their pistols, but decided against it. They knew better than to catch a case by trying to come to Manolo's defense. Troy applied the bracelets to Manolo's wrists and then pulled a search warrant from his back pocket.

"Fuck is you doing coming up in here? Fuck you looking for?" Manolo yelled.

"Turn this place inside out," Troy commanded as the police squad spread throughout the club.

Troy wanted to make it look good, so he didn't go to the safe right away. He searched the club for about twenty minutes before he discovered the safe that, of course, Tasha had already informed him of. "Jackpot, boys! Let's take him in to be processed," Troy announced. He placed the bricks in a duffel bag along with the money, and then headed out of the club.

Tasha looked at Halleigh and Mimi. The satisfaction on their faces was priceless, but now it was time for her to go collect their money. "Stay here and clear the club out. I'm going to get our cut now before Officer Troy gets any ideas. I'll come back in about an hour," she stated then left the club.

She drove toward Miller Road and parked her car in the empty shopping center lot. Just as planned, Troy was waiting for her. She eagerly hopped out of the car.

"I got to take ten thousand and two kilos of cocaine back to the station so that I can log it in as evidence," he informed her as she approached.

"What? You didn't tell me that," she protested.

"Look, my ass is the one who has to build this case against Manolo in order for him to do jail time. There's twenty thousand in there for you. You can also keep the rest of the dope. I can't do anything with that," he stated.

Tasha's eyes lit up when he said that. She knew that the eight bricks were as good as gold, so she shut up and accepted the deal. "Nice doing business with you, Troy," she stated with a wink.

"Very nice," he replied as he licked his lips and eyed her up and down. "Let me know if you'd like to do *it* again."

Tasha smirked. The sex was good, but it wasn't that damn good. She still hated cops, and she knew that she wouldn't make a habit of dealing with Troy. She hopped back into her vehicle and pulled away.

When she arrived back at the club, Mimi and Halleigh were waiting patiently for her. She was surprised that they had gotten rid of everyone so quickly.

"You get the money?" Mimi asked, the dollar signs practically forming in her eyes.

"Yeah, I got it. There are twenty stacks here and eight bricks," Tasha replied.

"What are we gon' do with some dope?" Halleigh asked.

"Don't worry about it. I'm gon' holla at my brother. He lives in New York. We're going to visit him there. We'll let things cool down before we come back," Tasha stated. "If we come back."

Tasha divided the cash by giving herself $8,000 and then giving Halleigh and Mimi $6,500 apiece. She figured she should get a little more for putting the plan together and fucking with Troy to carry it out. Mimi and Halleigh had no objections.

"Look, y'all. No one can know that we set up Manolo's arrest, so we just have to keep our mouths shut and let things die down. Then I promise you that everything will be fine," Tasha instructed.

Halleigh smiled and hugged Tasha tightly. "Thank you, Tash. Thank you so much," she stated.

Mimi was busy flicking through her money when she burst out laughing.

"What's so funny?" Halleigh asked with a frown.

Mimi shook her head and giggled some more. "Did y'all see Manolo's face when the police blew up his spot?" she asked. Halleigh and Tasha joined in on the laughter. "His ass was getting ready to cry when they put those handcuffs on him," Mimi stated, shaking her head.

"What goes around comes around," Halleigh stated. "I hope he rots in the mu'fucka."

"Let's get out of here," Tasha said as she rose from her seat. "We've got a long drive ahead of us." Tasha had changed her plans to fly to New York when she decided that she would take Mimi and Tasha with her. Leaving them in Flint was too risky. If they were with her, they couldn't talk.

The girls exited the club with a burden lifted from their heart. Manolo had taken advantage of each of them in their own way. As they pulled away from the club, they felt safe and secure in knowing that their betrayal would be a secret that would never leave those four walls.

Just as Tasha, Halleigh and Mimi drove away, Keesha came walking out of the club with envy in her eyes. She had just overheard the most valuable information she'd ever encountered. She knew it had to be worth something. Now she just had to figure out how she would use it to her advantage.